Alias

Mike Gold Mystery Book 5

a novel by

Phil Bookman

Tanya,
Keep reading!
Phil

Copyright © 2015 by Philip Bookman

ISBN-13: 978-1519318183
ISBN-10: 1519318189

Printed in the United States of America
First edition 2015

*To Barbie, alias Doris Barbara
and Bud, alias Milford Norman*

Also by Phil Bookman

Fiction

Slice (Mike Gold Mystery Series Book 4)
Riding the Tiger (Mike Gold Mystery Series Book 3)
Charisma (Mike Gold Mystery Series Book 2)
Opium (Mike Gold Mystery Series Book 1)

Non-Fiction

Attacking The Crown Jewels: how to protect your
business strategy against competitive threats

"*Although Smith, Jones, and Johnson are easy names to remember when there is no occasion to remember them, it is next to impossible to recollect them when they are wanted. How do criminals manage to keep a brand-new alias in mind? This is a great mystery.*"
Samuel Langhorne Clemens, alias Mark Twain
Life on the Mississippi

Chapter 1

Afterwards, Lisa Gold could not explain why she had done it. She used the cheeky line, "I was jealous of all the attention Mike was getting for his injuries." Lame, but it always got at least a smile. Sometimes she wondered if it might actually be true. Perhaps a little?

She wondered because what she did was so out of character for her. She was the cautious one, the "ready, aim, aim, aim, maybe fire" one. Her husband, Mike, was often more "ready, fire, aim." She was always still at the curb considering what to do when Mike was halfway across the street.

Lisa was driving along the Silverado Trail, the two-lane road that runs along the quiet east edge of Napa Valley. The busy Fourth of July weekend was over and Duncan Gold Vineyards, where she was general manager, had finally settled down from the holiday tourist crush. She had the Jeep's windows down and was enjoying the cooler-than-usual weather and admiring the gently rolling expanse of grapevines that carpeted the valley. Heading away from the winery she managed, Lisa turned onto Yountville Cross Road, cutting across to the western side of the narrow valley, the side that burst with touristy commercialism.

She was thinking—actually, it was more like daydreaming—about the lunch meeting she was going to, when she heard a loud pop. *Firecracker?* It sounded like it came from the vineyards on the left side of the road. As she braked, she heard three more pops in rapid succession. *Gunshots?*

Without hesitation, and later she would swear that it was without conscious thought, Lisa turned sharply left across the empty two lane road, crossed the shoulder, and headed down a narrow dirt access road through the vines. She bumped along for perhaps a hundred feet, when she came to a clearing opposite a weathered red barn with Brandetti Winery painted in large block white letters on its side.

Suddenly, a bald, bearded man emerged from the vines on her left. As he stumbled past the front of her car, another man followed from between the rows of vines. He had a gun in his hand and was striding purposefully towards the staggering bald man. As he raised the hand holding the pistol, Lisa got a clear view of his face. What she saw became etched in her memory. His face was distorted in a grimace of pure rage.

Lisa had one thought: *He's going to kill him now.* She gunned the engine, the Jeep lurched forward, and she slammed on the brakes. The car was now between the two men. The gunman extended his arm to shoot over the roof of the car. He was almost touching her door, so she slammed it open, throwing all her weight into the effort. The door hit his arm as he shot into the air.

As the shooter ran to his now collapsed victim, Lisa bolted from the car. Arm fully extended, the gunman calmly pointed his weapon at the cowering man's head. Lisa sprinted the few strides that separated them, leaped on the gunman's back, and they crashed in a heap on top of the prone victim.

The gun went off again. Lisa felt a sharp pain in her head. Everything was suddenly quiet. She tried to get up but only got to her knees. She was dizzy. Her vision was blurry and, when she felt her head, her hand came away bloody. Better to stay still for a while, she thought. Then she heard the sirens.

Chapter 2

Amy Wu, Kyle Rizzo and I sat in the shade on the front porch of Big Vic, the stately Victorian mansion that served as the owners' residence at Duncan Gold Vineyards, the Napa Valley winery my wife Lisa and I own with our partners, Jackie and Conrad Duncan.

The ironic thing about the partnership was that the whole thing had been Jackie Duncan's idea. She found the winery for sale and got her husband interested. Then he asked me if Lisa and I might be interested in being partners in the deal. I liked the idea of being a gentleman winery owner, strolling through vineyards and among barrels of wine. The last person to be convinced was Lisa, and I think she agreed because she knew how much I wanted to do it.

So we bought the place. Not long afterward, Lisa volunteered that she wanted a try at being general manager, a job at which she has excelled. Meanwhile, Jackie Duncan lost interest, too caught up in her Orange County society to come north to Napa Valley very often. I think Connie would have been around more often—he loved talking wine making and grape growing with Lisa and flew his own plane—if Jackie could just manage to show a bit of enthusiasm.

Regardless, both our families had roomy suites in Big Vic, and there was still plenty of room in the classy old gal for guests.

Rosa Ramos, our housekeeper, cook and Den Mother, had prepared a light lunch, a selection of cheeses, pâtés and fresh fruit, along with a sliced crusty French baguette and a chilled bottle of Duncan Gold Viognier.

Amy was the Wu in Kowalski-Wu Investigations, a private detective agency with whom I had a long relationship. Kyle Rizzo was one of their investigators. When Amy had asked for this meeting, she'd been a bit vague. All I knew was that they wanted to talk about something to do with the theft of 50 million dollars last year from the late Zack Zander's foundation. Amy and Kyle had driven to Napa Valley that morning from their office in Silicon Valley, two hours to the south.

Several years ago, Zack Zander had founded MySlice, an ingenious marriage of a pizza chain with social media. It soon became one of the hottest companies in Silicon Valley. In the process, Zack had become a billionaire. Along with three other MySlice executives, he had been murdered last year onboard his yacht, in Mexican waters off the coast of Baja California. I had then been hired to take over for him as CEO of MySlice.

One of the first acts I took as MySlice CEO was to engage Kowalski-Wu to investigate the executive murders, but they weren't working for the company any longer; that case was closed.

Amy looks like a tiny Chinese pixie. Her appearance and little girl voice cause people to underestimate her, often at their peril. She is smart, tough, and one of the best computer hackers on the planet.

Kyle is a thin, blue-eyed, blond haired, sunburned young man. He was a few years out of a special ops unit in Iraq that was responsible for providing security for top military brass. He too disarmed people with his aw shucks, Opie looks and manner.

After some appropriate small talk, which mainly centered on how I was recovering from my various injuries, there was a pause in the conversation. As we all nibbled and sipped, I waited for one of them to tell me more about why we were having this delightful get-together.

"Here's the short version, Mike," Amy said. "I found the 50 million dollars Angie Grey stole from Zack Zander's foundation. I know where it is. I also know who was in cahoots with Angie, and it wasn't Raul Rojas."

Huh! Angie Grey had been Zack Zander's vice president of human resources at MySlice. She had also headed up his charitable foundation. Angie quit MySlice shortly after I arrived, and disappeared along with 50 million dollars from the foundation. She had been found murdered in Guadalajara shortly thereafter.

Mexican authorities pinned her murder, as well as the murders of Zack and the others on his yacht, on Raul Rojas, a kingpin in the Los Hermanos drug cartel in Columbia. The official story was that the murders on Zack's yacht were part of Rojas's plot to steal the yacht so he could sell it. He also supposedly had a relationship of some sort with Angie Grey, and murdered her after she embezzled the 50 million for him. After his arrest, Rojas was himself killed in a crossfire between Mexican police and cartel soldiers intent on rescuing him from police custody.

Now Amy was telling me that Rojas had not been Angie Grey's accomplice in the embezzlement. Well, nothing about that whole crazy situation would surprise me at this point, so all I said was, "Who was it?"

"Tracy Luce," she said.

Well, well. Tracy Luce had been Zack's administrative assistant. She also left MySlice shortly after I arrived. In fact, as I now recalled, there were only a couple of days between Angie's and Tracy's departures. I also remembered hearing that Tracy was cold and aloof, and the only person at MySlice she had been at all friendly with, besides her boss Zack, had been Angie. And both Angie and Zack had been murdered. *Oh boy!*

I refilled everyone's wine glass, then spread some pâté on a slice of bread. "I think I'm ready for the long story," I said.

"Well, after the whole Rojas thing came out, your legal department referred the foundation's lawyer to us to try to track down the stolen 50 million."

"Wouldn't the FBI or DEA do that?" I said.

"The DEA told our client that even though Rojas was a cartel honcho, it wasn't drug money, so not their business," Amy said. "The FBI said that if the cartel had the money, it was more than likely long gone. They said they'd try, but it was pretty clear it was not a high priority. That's when we got on the case.

"I also didn't think there was any chance of getting the money back if the cartel had it. But maybe Rojas had stolen it for himself. I mean, the yacht-theft business was sort of an on-the-side thing, separate from his cartel activity. So maybe the plot with Angie Grey was too."

Amy nibbled a tiny morsel of cheese and sipped her wine. "We knew the bank and account number the money was wired to in Zurich, because that wire came from the foundation's bank. And right there, we got lucky. I was able to hack into the Zurich bank's system and get the date the account was opened. The name on the account was International Ebola Relief Fund. Totally bogus. It was set up in Lichtenstein by a nominee, a lawyer. It was a shell company set up to hide the identity of the real account owner.

"Then I hacked into the bank's security camera system. They have a camera in the lobby that covers the front door that takes a photo of the face of every person who enters. It's pretty cool, it tracks you, finds your face, and snaps a bunch of shots, then keeps the best one. They store them in the cloud, filed by date. They don't seem to ever delete them. So I looked at the photos for the date the account was opened.

"Sure enough, I recognized two of the people who came in that day. Angie Grey I knew because we had investigated her murder for you. The other gal I had seen sitting outside your office that first meeting we had at MySlice, but I couldn't remember her name. One call to your assistant and I had it: Tracy Luce."

I tipped my glass to Amy, acknowledging her brilliant work. "Maybe they were both working with Rojas," I said.

"That's possible, but stay with me while we follow the money. From Zurich, it was quickly wired to a dozen different banks in a dozen countries. Those accounts were also for shell companies. Each of those companies was set up using a different name in a different country by a different local attorney. The only name and address associated with an account were the attorney's. But I could hack into the international bank wire system well enough to follow the money from account to account. There are codes in the wire data that let you do that, and I wasn't changing any data, just reading it, so I was in and out before my exploit was detected.

"The last stop was a bank in the Cook Islands, where all the funds came back together. That's one of the last places where they're still really strict about bank secrecy and it's also safe to keep your money. I mean, there are places in the world, especially in Asia and Africa, where they don't cooperate with legal requests for banking data, but you might just as well burn your money as trust them with it. Anyway, there the money was," Amy said. "But how to get it back?"

"Couldn't you just hack in like you did with Glen Harper?" I said.

Glen Harper had been chief of staff for U.S. Senator Sonya Rivera. He had gotten some legislation passed that significantly benefitted MySlice during its startup years, which became known inside the company as the Fed Deal. In exchange, he had received several million dollars in kickbacks. After I came to MySlice, I unraveled that scheme.

In an effort to right the wrong without jeopardizing the company, I had gotten Harper fired and had Amy wire his ill-gotten gains somewhere where the money would do some real good. My attempt to balance the cosmic scales of justice that way led to my almost getting blown up, the injuries from which I was still recovering. But I'll get to that later.

"With Harper, I knew all about him," Amy said. "He was a government employee; there was information about him everywhere. So all I had to do was log into his bank account. I had already hacked into his email and knew that password. Sure enough, he used the same user name and password for online banking. When you wire a few million dollars online, you have to answer some security questions, but I knew more about Harper than his mother, so that was no problem. As far as the bank's online system was concerned, I was Glen Harper.

"But the Cook Islands account was another story. I got read-only access to the account easily enough, but it was in the name of Amanda Miller, not Tracy Luce. Probably an alias, but just in case it wasn't, I tried to track her down online. There are thousands of Amanda Millers in the United States. Way too many to wade through. Without more information about her, I couldn't just hack into her account and wire the money back home like we did with Harper."

"What happened to Tracy Luce?" I said.

"Funny you should ask," Amy said. "She vanished without a trace about the same time Angie and the money took off.

"Anyway, for several frustrating weeks, I tried social engineering. But the Cook Islands bank staff were as tight-lipped as I've ever seen. And bribery didn't work either. When that stuff doesn't work remotely, it's time to do it in person, and I was thinking about sending Kyle down there to see if he could pry something loose.

"Meanwhile, I was monitoring the account activity every day, and while we were dithering about whether or not to send Kyle, 45 million was wired to the account of Manville Enterprises in Samoa. That's actually a real company, which was not a good thing. It's usually a sign that the money's going to be well laundered. So, with the client's okay, Kyle flew right off to Samoa."

Amy nodded at Kyle, and he took his cue. "I hitchhiked from the airport to a little village called Tulula, where Manville is located. I had a backpack, dirty jeans and t-shirt, and well-worn hiking boots. I tried to look like another scruffy wanderer, the kind you find all over the world sleeping on beaches. Which is what I did." He described Tulula and what he'd learned about the Manville operation after a few days of roaming around and chatting up the locals. Fortunately, he found that English seemed to be everyone's second language.

"While I was gathering intel, Amy was online digging into Manville Enterprises. We found out that Amanda Miller is an American, a recent arrival, and had become a partner in Manville Enterprises. She runs their property management outfit. I got a lot of photos of her with my phone. That was easy, Tulula being so small and isolated. I even managed to cop a glass she was drinking from in a café so we could lift some fingerprints. Then I came home. That was a few days ago."

It was Amy's turn again. "Since then, we've been trying to track down Amanda Miller. I've run her prints through every database I could. No joy. Same for her photos. Then Kyle had a wild idea. What if Amanda was Tracy with a new face? So that's why we're here."

"Sorry, I don't get it," I said.

Amy grinned her sweet smarty-pants-little-girl grin. "We'd like your permission to get whatever photos of Tracy Luce MySlice has. We couldn't find any anywhere else. She was completely off-the grid."

Before I could respond, my cell phone rang. I glanced at the caller ID. It was Jeff Ryder, the county sheriff. I started to let it go to voice mail, thought better of it, held up my hand to signal that I needed to take the call, and hit the green button.

"It's Lisa, Mike," Sheriff Ryder said. "She's being taken to the ER. She's been shot!"

Chapter 3

Fifteen minutes later, we pulled up to the emergency room entrance at Queen of the Valley Medical Center. Amy drove—I was not yet medically cleared for driving—while I navigated and Kyle sat in back. I knew the hospital well, as I had used their services several times over the last few months.

As I tore into the ER waiting room, I saw Sheriff Ryder talking to a woman in green scrubs.

"Jeff..." I shouted.

"She's okay, Mike, she's okay," he said.

Lisa and I had gotten to know Jeff Ryder pretty well over the past few years. I later learned that when he arrived at the crime scene and saw Lisa being loaded into an ambulance on a gurney, he turned the crime scene over to a detective and tore off after the ambulance.

The doctor told me that Lisa had a minor head wound. The bullet had creased her scalp and just nicked her skull. He said that, although wounds like that bleed like crazy, it was nothing to worry about. They'd stitched her up, given her some blood and an antibiotic, and she was in recovery. I could see her in a few minutes.

I saw that Jeff had tears in his eyes and I lost it. I just started bawling with pent-up emotion. Mainly relief.

I was sitting next to Lisa's bed when she woke up.

"Hi," I said softly.

"Oh, hi," she said dreamily.

I just held her hand for a while. I thought about how much time Lisa had spent next to my hospital bed just a few months ago as I recovered from what we now called the Halloween Explosion.

Time to explain that. The explosion occurred last year at the MySlice staff Halloween picnic. This was shortly after Senator Sonya Rivera had fired her chief of staff Glen Harper for his part in the Fed Deal, and he had drained millions in kickbacks that he had gotten from MySlice from his bank account. Harper showed up at the picnic in a Darth Vader costume, walked up to MySlice executive Jack Doyle, and detonated explosives he had taped to his chest.

Harper and Doyle were killed instantly. I was standing right behind Harper at the time, and miraculously survived. Fortunately, we were far enough away from others so that no one else was injured.

While there was evidence that Doyle knew Harper, no one knew why he had done it. Except me. I had unearthed the Fed Deal and kickbacks, the plot he and Zack had cooked up along with two other MySlice founding executives. Those three had been killed on Zack's yacht. I only realized Jack was also a part of the scheme when I heard Harper say "Fuck you Doyle" the instant before he blew himself and Jack to pieces. I had not shared my realization with anyone else except Lisa and my shrink.

My injuries were extensive. I had multiple surgeries, and was still having daily physical therapy. I had a concussion and memory loss of the events of that day; the memory returned as the concussion healed. I have a new right knee, a titanium rod in my left leg, and a transplanted tendon from a cadaver in my right elbow. Those are just the major items; the list of the other repairs to my bones and soft tissue is lengthy.

More, it had been my clever plan that led to Harper being old, unemployed and broke. He must have assumed Jack was the one who had cost him his job and his retirement savings. It was my fault Jack Doyle and Glen Harper were dead. I had played god and my suffering was my own fault. So I was engaged in ongoing psychotherapy in addition to my daily physical therapy.

That was why I was living at the winery. Napa Valley was far enough away from MySlice headquarters in Silicon Valley to prevent me from sneaking off to the office or calling meetings at my home. I was still able to perform my job as CEO. I had a great executive team and an understanding board, the latter buttressed by the outstanding financial results the company was producing.

"Go ahead," Lisa said. "Ask me why I did it."

"Okay, why in the world did you do it?" I said.

"I was jealous of all the attention you've been getting for your injuries," she said with a mischievous smile.

"You've been lying there rehearsing that line, haven't you?" I said.

I let a nurse know that Lisa was awake and found Jeff Ryder on his phone in the waiting room. When we got to Lisa's bedside, a nurse was adjusting medical gadgets and showing Lisa where the call button was.

Lisa was sipping water from a plastic cup through a straw. "She can have as much water as she wants," the nurse said, showing me where the pitcher was. "But just sips, honey," she said to Lisa.

The nurse eyed Sheriff Ryder, who was in uniform, warily. "I'll only stay a few minutes," he said.

When the nurse was gone, Jeff pulled up a visitor's chair and we both sat at Lisa's bedside.

"I'd like you to tell me what happened," he said.

I looked at Jeff skeptically. "I know what you're thinking, Mike. But we'll get a formal statement tomorrow and you can have your lawyer there. This is just for me. It's as off the record as you can be with a cop."

So Lisa told Jeff what had happened from the time she heard the first shot until the ambulance took her away from the scene. He listened attentively, asked no questions, took no notes.

When she was finished, he nodded a few times and said, "Okay, here's what I know so far. The shooter's was Giuseppe Brandetti. The guy he was chasing is named Sam Jones. Brandetti leased the barn and called it Brandetti Winery. He and Jones had a business meeting this morning to try to settle a legal dispute, something to do with the winery. They met in an office that's inside the barn, along with their attorneys.

"Apparently they took a break around noon, just before you drove up. Brandetti and Jones decide to take a stroll together through the vineyards while the lawyers get on their phones to do other lawyering.

"Soon they hear yelling. One of the lawyers looks out of the meeting room and sees Brandetti running into his office. Brandetti comes out with a gun. Jones runs out of the barn, Brandetti follows, they hear shots and one of them calls 9-1-1. That's pretty much all I know at this point."

"How are they?" Lisa said.

"Jones took at least three hits. He was unconscious when the EMTs arrived and had lost a lot of blood. They told me he was in critical condition but should pull through. In fact," he said, looking around as if suddenly realizing it, "he's around here somewhere."

"The other guy?" she said.

"Brandetti didn't make it. It looks like when you tackled him and you both fell onto Jones, the gun went off and passed through his heart, out his back, and grazed your head." Jeff looked Lisa squarely in the eyes and his voice became low and solemn. "If you hadn't come along and done what you did, he would have killed Jones. You saved his life."

"So the bullet bounced off your skull, and only the bullet was damaged," I said after Jeff left.

"You repeat that line, bub, and you'll be in big trouble," Lisa said.

I smiled. She was feeling much better.

"Now I know how it feels," she said.

"How what feels?"

"I mean how you felt after the Halloween Explosion. That you were responsible for Jack Doyle's death and Glen Harper's death."

"You weren't responsible for Brandetti's death or Jones being shot. Brandetti was responsible for both. You saved Jones's life."

"*My* Spock knows that," Lisa said seriously. "But *my* Kirk is still working on it.

Chapter 4

Once we both realized that Lisa was going to be fine, we turned our attention to what could become a mob scene at Duncan Gold Vineyards. It was a good distraction from our churning emotions.

When I had been nearly pulverized in the Halloween Explosion, Lisa put the word out that I was to have no visitors. This was in part in direct response to what my doctors told her, but more she-cat Lisa fiercely protecting her seriously wounded mate. Except for our kids, Lisa enforced this unmercifully until I was transferred from Stanford Hospital to recuperate at the winery. Over the months of my recuperation, I'd had quite a few visitors at Big Vic, but Rosa was always hovering to be sure none overstayed their welcome. Being in Napa Valley, a two-hour drive from Silicon Valley, created a self-regulating flow of visitors. Had I been home in Los Gatos, minutes from MySlice headquarters and near lots of friends and family, it would be too easy for folks to come over to the house. A trip up to Napa at least required some forethought and a call ahead of time.

This would be different. They had been able to stitch up Lisa's head minutes after she arrived at the ER. She would only spend one night in the hospital. The doctor said she needed to take it easy, watch out for dizziness, and be very careful walking, especially stairs. No lifting, no driving. For a week. But she would soon be back to normal.

The "death in the vineyards" story would probably have been good for one news cycle, and likely only locally, if Lisa hadn't been married to someone with my notoriety. Instead, it was instant national news. Ted Trotter had already made it the lead story of his CNN segments, juxtaposing Lisa's heroics with all the MySlice brouhaha from last year: the yacht murders of Zack and the other executives, the murder of former MySlice executive Angie Grey soon thereafter, topped off with the Halloween Explosion that took the lives of MySlice executive Jack Doyle and Senate staffer Glen Harper and left me with a shattered body.

In the past, Lisa had stayed out of the limelight. Now Trotter was calling us the "golden power couple" and other cable news stations were climbing on the bandwagon. By that evening, it was starting to sound like Lisa and I were action heroes in some sort of Silicon Valley-Napa Valley video game. Meanwhile, Brandetti and Jones were lost in the shuffle.

Mid-afternoon, I got a call from José, the tasting room manager, that reporters and gawkers were descending on the winery. I made a command decision. Amy and Kyle were still in the waiting room. They had already told me in no uncertain terms that they were staying overnight and would be available for any help we needed. So I asked them to go back to Duncan Gold Vineyards, shoo all the outsiders away, close the gates to the long drive that led from the Silverado Trail to the parking lot, and put up the "closed" sign. Then I called the tasting room and let them know that they were closing for the day.

By early evening, Lisa was raring to go. She is nothing if not resilient. We'd watched the news coverage together, and Amy had called to let us know that they had executed the plan and were now doing guard duty at the gate. News folks do not discourage easily.

I wanted to close the winery for a week. "Nonsense," she said, "this is a great marketing opportunity." Lisa went into planning mode.

Getting into a hospital is a lot easier than getting out. There seems to be a nearly endless litany of things that need to be done after they tell you that you can go home. And it seems that none of those things are a priority for the staff. Ah, well.

So it was about noon Thursday when Amy drove us up to the Duncan Gold front gate. As expected, it was a mob scene, with dozens of cars parked on the shoulders of the Silverado Trail. There was a big sign across the gateway that said, "Special Event Today—Club Members Only." A half a dozen rent-a-cops, wearing yellow windbreakers with "Event Staff" in bold black letters across the back, were on duty. Two tasting room staff members were sitting behind a folding table, armed with iPads equipped with credit card readers. They were signing up people who wanted to get into the winery—news folks and the merely curious—as new wine club members. They were doing a brisk business.

The security people were answering questions, doing some traffic control, and one was letting in the cars of wine club members, most of whom had just signed up.

Lisa looked very pleased as we were waved through.

There were more event staff in our very large parking lot, which was jammed. The tasting room staff—today was an all-hands-on-deck day—had set up long tables outside so they could serve the crowd that was overflowing Little Vic, the smaller Victorian that housed the winery offices and tasting room. Across the lot, a section of the parking lot in front of Big Vic had been roped off, and a special event person was politely redirecting visitors, especially members of the press, who had difficulty understanding the "private residence" signs.

Last night, we had worked out the wording for Lisa's "party line" about the incident. This morning, one of Lisa's staff had gotten cards printed that said, "Ms. Gold reacted as anyone would when she encountered a life-threatening emergency. Her thoughts are with Mr. Jones, and she wishes him a speedy recovery. Her minor injury is healing well. She will be giving no further statements about this incident." The cards were given to the tasting room staff and security people, who were instructed to read from them whenever it seemed appropriate. There were plenty of extra cards around—we'd had printed five hundred—and everyone was told to hand them out freely, especially to the press.

We were greeted on the front porch by a sight that was guaranteed to lift our spirits: there stood our son Andy and his wife Melissa, with our first and only grandchild in her arms. Grandma Lisa wanted to hold baby Brian. Andy and Melissa were concerned about Grandma's head, which had been shaved and sported an impressive turban-like bandage. But soon it was all sorted out and Lisa was happily sitting on a rocking chair with her grandson cradled in her arms.

Andy said that his younger brother, Alan, had just called from Napa airport and was on his way in a taxi. Our lawyer, Annie Oakley, was driving up from Silicon Valley with Lisa's sister Julie, and they would arrive mid-afternoon. Big Vic was a huge old Victorian, but it was filling up.

Amy and Kyle had stayed in a couple of Big Vic's guest rooms last night, and would be leaving for home later in the day. As Rosa oohed and aahed over the baby and consulted with Lisa about meals and room assignments, I went over to Amy, who was standing outside her car.

"I can't thank you and Kyle enough for your help," I said.

"We're glad we were here to help," she said.

"About that question you asked, about getting photos MySlice may have of Tracy Luce? I'll let the IT guys know to help you with that. I'll call right away and set it up."

"Thanks."

"Let me know what happens."

"Sure." Amy said. "Our client knows we're getting your help. So it's okay to talk to you."

At 4:00 p.m., a detective arrived to take Lisa's formal statement with our lawyer, Annie Oakley, in attendance. Annie had explained that they had to get her official version of events, and Lisa and I had long ago learned that it was best to talk to the police with a lawyer present. For all the police knew, Lisa had driven up, taken Brandetti's gun and started shooting people.

Less than an hour after the detective left, Sheriff Ryder called.

"Mike, this is informal, but I just talked to the DA. Lisa's story agrees with the two lawyers' accounts and the forensic evidence. Of course, no charges will be filed. Your lawyer will be notified Monday."

"Thanks, Jeff," I said.

"Your gal's still a hero, Mike."

Alvin Baxter watched the CNN "death in the vineyards" report. He was transfixed by the photos of Sam Jones. *Got you at last, you bastard.*

Chapter 5

The editor of the *San Jose Mercury News* must have decided that his newspaper was going to be the authoritative source for the "death in the vineyards" story, because they ran a lengthy piece that Saturday about Giuseppe Brandetti. This went far beyond the five-sentence summary about the "vineyard gunman" that all the other news outlets seemed to have picked up off the Associated Press wire.

According to the article, Giuseppe Brandetti had been born Joseph Brandet in Houston, Texas. Joe came from a long line of petty thieves and conmen. He proudly told the story of how his great-grandfather had gotten the family name to his Houston acquaintances. It seems Great-Grandad had been hiding out from the law in west Texas, working on a ranch for a man named Brandt. It wasn't long before he decided he was not cut out for ranch work and took off.

Being a wanted man, Great-Grandad decided it would be prudent to ditch his real name, and, being a man of limited imagination, took his former boss's name. Being also a man of limited education, he misspelled it, and so the Brandet family name came into being.

Joe told this story to his circle of Houston-area small businessmen who gathered at a private club that excluded anyone who wasn't white, male and Christian. They drank, smoked cigars, and guffawed as the swapped stories about good-old-boys they knew who had gotten away with all manner of misdeeds, public and private. Joe Brandet fit right in.

Joe had been what was characterized by those who knew him then as a "troubled youth," growing up in a rundown section of Houston. Somewhere in his inauspicious gene pool he had gotten some academic ability, and had somehow managed to graduate from the University of Houston with a B.S. in chemistry. Joe thought that B.S. was a great pun, and determined that he would go through life capitalizing on the bullshit claim that he was a chemist.

After college, Joe borrowed a few thousand dollars from various friends and started a company that provided supplies to the oil wildcatting industry in Texas. Wildcatters are fundamentally gamblers who drill wells away from established oil fields in the hope of finding a gusher. His Houston warehouse mainly contained out-of-date, discontinued, and often no-longer-legal materials his larger, more legitimate competitors needed to unload. It was also said that he took deliveries from truckers who somehow found extra goods left on their trucks after making deliveries elsewhere. Joe sold to those who liked his low prices and turned a blind eye to the fudged paperwork.

Joe Brandet had come to the Napa Valley two years ago, after selling his Houston business. Though it was doubtful there was any Italian in his ancestry, he immediately legally changed his name to Giuseppe Brandetti, apparently believing that was a better moniker for a wine baron, which he was determined to become. Giuseppe the chemist would now devote his skills to the chemistry of winemaking, or so he would tell anyone who would listen. One acquaintance commented about his ridiculous attempt at an Italian accent with his Texas drawl.

Brandetti's arrival in Napa was marred by a flood of legal actions stemming from the sale of his Houston business. The acquiring company claimed that there were substantial debts that weren't on the books; equipment that was supposedly owned turned out to be leased, with payments in arrears; a key patented lubricant for oil well drills that Joe the chemist had developed and was the main reason for the deal turned out to not work very well.

Brandetti's method of dealing with the lawsuits filed in Houston was to ignore them. This led to default judgements against him, but, try though they might, his creditors could find no appreciable assets in his name to seize in order to satisfy their claims.

Meanwhile, Giuseppe had found a property on the Yountville Cross that had a very large, unused barn. He cut a deal to lease the barn and a parking area adjacent to it, with rights to use a private access road as a driveway. The surrounding acres of vines were not part of the deal. He told his landlord he was going to use the barn for experimental winemaking.

Soon the old barn was bustling with contractors. It was cleaned out and the exterior was refurbished. A few offices, bathrooms and a tasting room were constructed inside, taking up about half the barn. The other half soon sported racks of wine barrels and an array of winemaking equipment. A sign appeared on the Yountville Cross at the foot of the driveway proclaiming that Brandetti Vineyards was open.

There were a few small problems. None of the work on the barn had permits. Giuseppe was not licensed to sell wine, offer tastings, or run any other business from his rented barn. This did not matter to Giuseppe, who was busy buying cheap surplus grapes from wherever he could and using a local crush-to-bottle plant to make wine from them. He also bought cut-rate wine in bulk from volume producers in the Central Valley, which he also had bottled. In a few short weeks, the Brandetti Vineyards label proudly appeared on cases of old and new wine stored in that old barn.

Brandetti spent his time in the tasting room, regaling naïve tourists with completely fabricated stories of how he had formulated his blends. He gave each blend a catchy name and made up a heartwarming story about it. The rosé—he really had no idea what was inside the bottles, he went strictly by color—was "Brittany's Blush," named, he'd sadly intone, for his sweet soulmate who was taken from him so young by a tragic illness. However, the Texans who knew him said that, though he was a great hit-and-run ladies' man, he had never had anything resembling a relationship, and the reporter could find no evidence any such Brittany had ever existed.

He engaged a local lawyer who was gifted in his ability to repeatedly delay government proceedings brought against Brandetti Vineyards. When those tactics ran their course, Giuseppe would humbly and sincerely agree to remedy his unintended transgressions. He would then completely ignore each such agreement. And the process would repeat.

So Giuseppe Brandetti, self-style vintner extraordinaire, pedaled his swill on unsuspecting tourists while staying one step ahead of the repeated efforts by various representatives of local government agencies to shut him down.

Giuseppe Brandetti had funded his venture by taking on a silent partner. Sam Jones was a Silicon Valley investor who, like so many who had acquired wealth in that tech mecca, was lured to Napa Valley by the romance and caché of vineyards and winemaking. Foregoing his usually thorough due diligence, Jones succumbed to Brandetti's considerable charm, and put up two million dollars for half ownership.

It did not take long for Jones to regret his uncharacteristically impulsive investment. Their agreement specified that Brandetti was to draw a modest salary, which he in fact did. But he leased a luxury condo and Cadillac Escalade for himself, both in the name of the business. Brandetti had assured Jones that he had an option to lease the vineyards surrounding the barn, and would do so as soon as Jones's check cleared. In fact, no such option existed. Not to mention the seemingly unending problems with the local authorities.

Try though he might, Jones could not get the monthly financial statements he was due from Brandetti, who kept changing banks and could not seem to find a satisfactory bookkeeper or accountant. After several months of putting up with Brandetti's excuses and delaying tactics, and weary of driving for two hours to meet with him only to have the meeting cancelled at the last minute by some sort of emergency Giuseppe simply had to attend to personally, an exasperated Sam Jones filed suit for fraud and breach of contract.

After months of delays by Brandetti's wily lawyer, Jones prevailed in court. Brandetti was ordered to sell off all company assets to satisfy the two million dollar judgement, plus pay Jones's legal costs. Brandetti humbly agreed—he had no choice—and then happily ignored the judgement.

More legal proceedings ensued, during which it was revealed that Brandetti had been up to his old tricks. The company essentially owned nothing; all the furniture and fancy winemaking equipment listed on his balance sheet as assets was leased, and, of course, payments were in arrears. While he was still moving company money from bank to bank to keep it out of his partner's reach, it came out that he had used a half million dollars of it to settle his Houston legal problems.

Finally, an exasperated judge ordered the parties to get together and reach some sort of a final settlement. He told Brandetti in no uncertain terms that he would spend time in jail if he was uncooperative. And, for good measure, he ordered Brandetti Vineyards to immediately cease selling wine and offering tastings.

That was the meeting that was in recess when the shooting incident occurred. And that was why the sign for Brandetti Vineyards was no longer at the end of the driveway onto the Yountville Cross when Lisa Gold turned into it on that fateful day.

Ted Trotter had covered the tech industry as a freelance writer and blogger for years before he became an all-purpose pundit on CNN. I'm sure he used his close ties to the Mercury-News to get the interview he ran on Sunday with the reporter who did their piece on Brandetti. This gave that titillating story national exposure and gave legs to the whole "death in the vineyards" narrative.

Sunday afternoon, Lisa and I watched Trotter's interview with the Mercury-News reporter in our suite in Big Vic. We'd politely sent everyone home. We told the kids and Julie to get on with their lives, and they could see that Lisa was fine.

Lisa had spent a lot of time on the phone during the weekend reassuring friends that she had just had a scratch and that the whole thing was less dramatic than the news reports. Duncan Gold Vineyards was still chaotic and this was not the time to visit, thank you.

"We have to do something about this zoo," I said, gesturing towards the window overlooking the parking lot and Little Vic.

"I agree," Lisa said. "We got enough of a marketing pop. The staff is getting worn out. Do you think I should make a statement to the press?"

And you're not tired? I thought. Wise husband that I am, I said, "I don't think so. Let's stick to what you said on that card. We don't want you to be the story, right?"

Lisa sighed. "You're right. So what should we do?"

"I have two ideas. First, I think we should go home. Without you here, the gawkers will leave the zoo, and things will get back to normal. The last few days have shown me that I'm recovered enough to get back to the office. It's time for that. I can always get physical therapy near home."

"But you're not cleared for driving yet," she said.

She knows that's bogus. "I bet if I asked, I would be. And I can always get a ride if I need to."

"So you'd fly home with me?" she said with that sly grin I love so much.

Lisa knows I cannot handle small planes. The many crafty ways I avoid flying with her are part of our ongoing duet. But this time I didn't have to resort to subterfuge. "I think when the doctor told you not to drive, that included flying."

"But I'll be so cooped up."

"So see the doctor when we get home and get cleared to drive," I said.

"You're just spoiled because you have a fleet of jets at your disposal," Lisa said.

True. MySlice had a small fleet of Gulfstreams. Those I flew in just fine.

Lisa looked pouty. Something else was bothering her. *Oh, of course.* "You can get back to your hairdresser and work out what you'll do until that patch of hair grows back," I said. In the hospital, Lisa seemed astonished that none of the doctors or nurses could tell her how long it would take for her hair to grow in. In fact, they seemed bewildered by what, to their patient, was the most important question about her condition.

Lisa shrugged. "What's your second idea?" she said, not yet conceding my first.

"It's time to change the subject," I said. "Let's get the newsies to focus on something other than you."

"Now that Ted Trotter's run the story on CNN, they'll be all over Brandetti," she said.

"Which helps. I think it's time to get them to look at Mr. Jones, too," I said.

"Do you know something I don't?"

"Not a thing. But, after all, he was Brandetti's target and he's still in critical care. Why was Brandetti shooting at him? What's his backstory?"

"How do we do that?"

"Easy," I said. "Ted Trotter still owes me. So I'll ask him."

I had been instrumental in helping Ted Trotter graduate from Silicon Valley tech blogger-muckraker to featured CNN commentator. I did that by feeding him inside information about the MySlice executive murders last year. So I called Ted and suggested the direction his current reporting might take. He understood.

Chapter 6

By the time the front gate to Duncan Gold Vineyards was thrown open Monday morning, Lisa and I were gone. Tasting room operations were quickly back to normal. Two roving security folks in civilian dress were still around, and they still had a supply of those little cards to hand out as needed, but Twitter had announced our departure and the need for both the guards and the cards quickly evaporated.

As we rode home in the limo, Lisa started telling me what she would be doing during the week. I told her it didn't sound like what the doctor meant when he said, "take it easy."

"But that was last Wednesday," she said. "Tomorrow's Tuesday. My week will be up."

The engineer in me was not to be denied. Fool that I am, I plunged ahead. "That conversation was late Wednesday. So your week is up late tomorrow."

Lisa's right eyebrow shot up, a sure warning that I was on thin ice. Then she decided to take pity on me. She took her phone out of her purse, called her internist's office, and managed to get squeezed in for an appointment for first thing Wednesday morning.

"There," she said. "I'll be a good girl until Wednesday morning, sitting quietly at home until she clears me. But you are going to work tomorrow. I don't want you around the house hovering over me all day."

I wanted desperately to hire someone to help Lisa tomorrow, but I knew even suggesting it would be taking my life in my hands. And I had to admit she seemed just fine. So I stifled that impulse and took solace in my small victory. "Yes, ma'am," I said. "Thank you, ma'am."

Then I got on the phone. I called my doctor's office and arranged to have a prescription for physical therapy faxed to the clinic I'd used in the past. I also made a doctor's appointment for the following week to get checked up and cleared to drive. I pointedly did not make an effort to get "squeezed in." My forbearance was lost on Lisa, but at least I got to feel smug.

We caught Ted Trotter's segment on CNN that evening. He had more to say about Giuseppe Brandetti, including a couple of recorded video clips of comments by people who knew him. He painted Brandetti as a blowhard and scoundrel, and implied that he would not be missed.

As was his trademark, Ted ended his piece with provocative questions, intoning, "Who is Sam Jones? And why did Giuseppe Brandetti try to kill him?"

"Odd that he would say that," Lisa said. "I think I heard you ask those very same questions yesterday."

"I may have made one or two small suggestions when I talked to Ted," I said. That earned me a sweet kiss.

Chapter 7

As I walked into MySlice headquarters, just off Winchester Boulevard in Los Gatos and a few minutes from my house, I was the subject of stares and murmurs. This was not just the usual CEO sighting. To most of them over the many months I had been rehabbing at the winery, I had been the phantom CEO, whose presence was felt mainly through emails and the occasional teleconference.

Marty Geller, Chief Technology Officer of MySlice and my best friend, had picked me up that morning to give me a lift to work. He brought with him a MySlice shirt—tomato red, long-sleeved—with "He's Alive!" emblazoned across the back. I dutifully wore it into the office that day.

My admin, Nora Coleman, greeted me with a big hug, which she followed up by saying, "Everything's been just humming along. Now all hell will break loose around here!"

In truth, everything had been humming along just fine. Chief Operating Officer Paco Cruz had pizza ops, which is what we called the pizza side of the business, running like a well-oiled machine. His aggressive plan for new pizzeria openings was right on target. Other innovations in the menu and the new pop-up outlets were clicking with our customers. Quarter after quarter, he had beat Wall Street consensus estimates for revenue and earnings. Paco needed no help from me.

VP of Marketing Megan Ortiz had stepped up her game after Jack Doyle was killed in the Halloween Explosion. As a CEO, I usually found some way to have someone between me and the marketing folks, whose work I appreciated but who also tended to drive me to distraction. So I had put Jack Doyle between me and Megan when I took over at MySlice. But she had won me over, and, after Jack's death, I was content to have her report directly to me.

After the Halloween Explosions, we had needed a new marketing campaign. The previous campaign, "Pepperoni isn't Guacamole," revolved around a tongue-in-cheek feud between Jack Doyle, who was instrumental in founding MySlice, and then newcomer Paco Cruz, who had previously been at the helm of the Paco's Picante chain of Mexican restaurants he had founded. Jack's death put an end to that, too.

Megan and her staff came up with "Changing the World, One Slice at a Time." This was first and foremost a smart-ass send up of the Silicon Valley rubric in which every startup feels compelled to claim to be disruptive, open, innovative, and changing the world. One subtheme of the campaign featured MySlice staff saying "We just want to make good pizza" in response to Paco exhorting them to change the world. Another focused on our Slice University's program to help middle income minority Americans become MySlice franchisees. Still another showcased all the cools things you could do with your SliceBank.

The SliceBank had been MySlice's breakthrough innovation. Your SliceBank account was accessible on the internet and through the MySlice app. You could add slices to your SliceBank account, charged to your credit card. You could use your SliceBank to pay for food and drink at any MySlice location. You could also "slice" your friends on your handheld or on Facebook, sending a slice from your SliceBank to theirs. You could tag a slice with an emoticon when you sent it. People started slicing each other for all sorts of reasons. Say "hi" with a slice. Say "I'm sorry" with a slice. Say "I love you" with a slice. You could even contribute slices from your SliceBank to a charity's SliceBank. Most of these charities then used the slices to feed the poor, truly changing the world one slice at a time.

The new marketing campaign had been an instant winner, and it looked like it could be used for a long time.

Marty and I were eating lunch in the company cafeteria. I had taken a circuitous route there from my office to increase the opportunities for CEO sightings. Three weeks ago, I'd given up the cane I had been using, and my gait was pretty smooth now, though I still tired easily. My "He's Alive" shirt seemed to be a hit, and I got a lot of waves, nods, smiles and a few hugs and handshakes.

Marty confirmed that his wife, Ruth, had dropped in at our house to have lunch with Lisa. She was part of the babysitting conspiracy I had surreptitiously organized. Ruth would be relieved mid-afternoon by Lisa's sister,

Julie, who would come right over after the school where she taught let out. I knew Lisa would not be fooled by my cunning, but chances were she'd pretend to be.

"Lisa was sure unlucky," Marty said as we sat down with our trays of pizza and Diet Cokes.

This was the Marty I knew and loved. After the Halloween Explosion, when everyone else was saying how lucky I had been to not just have survived but to have such a positive prognosis, he had said the same thing to me: "You were sure unlucky."

This was Marty's way of making it easier for us to talk about something painful. I played along. Besides, if I didn't, he'd keep working what he thought of as a great gag until I did. "I thought she was very lucky," I said. "A half inch or so to the side, and that bullet could have killed her."

"Lucky would be her passing by a minute before the shots were fired," he said. "Lucky would be her getting a flat tire before she got there."

We both worked on our pizza for a while. According to the universal rules of cafeteria seating, we had been granted the mandatory executive 10 foot buffer from other diners. So our conversation had privacy.

"I was so scared," I said, barely getting the words out.

Marty nodded slowly. "I understand." He looked me in the eye, then looked away a bit awkwardly. I suddenly felt a lot better than I had in days.

Lisa was okay. I was done licking my wounds. I was feeling frisky and more than ready to dive back into work. I started planning my travel schedule. I was going to show everyone that the MySlice CEO was 100% back in action.

Chapter 8

When I got back after lunch, Kyle Rizzo was waiting outside my office door. He was sort of bouncing in place, his visitor badge hopping around on the chain around his neck. The phrase "jumping out of his skin" came to mind. As I went past her desk, my gatekeeper Nora looked at me and shook her head. "You've got time for this antsy guy if you want to see him," she said.

Kyle followed me into my office and closed the door. "We got her!" he said, pumping his fist in the air triumphantly. I realized he had a flash drive in his hand. A sword would have fit his mood better.

"I'm happy for you," I said.

Ignoring my snarkiness, he plunged ahead. "Amanda Johnson is Tracy Luce, and I can prove it. Let me show you."

He came around to my side of the desk and stuck the flash drive into a USB port on my laptop. While Windows scanned the new interloper for viruses, he previewed what we'd be viewing.

"Your IT guys used photo scanning software to search network backups since MySlice started. They came up with dozens of photos that included good shots of Tracy."

That made sense. Until she left last year, Tracy Luce had been Zack Zander's admin since he'd started MySlice. So she'd be in a lot of photos.

"We compared the photos I had of Amanda Miller with Tracy's. First we worked with the face." He pointed to side-by-side head shots on the large monitor I had hooked up to my laptop.

"They don't look at all alike," I said.

"I'm sure she had extensive plastic surgery. But even so, some things usually don't change. Like the size of the head and neck. And the position of the ear canal relative to the eyes. Things like that."

As I watched, the two images rotated in three dimensions. The skin and hair disappeared, replaced by colored contour lines. Then the two images were superimposed. It was like watching Abby Sciuto do her magic on NCIS.

Sure enough, Kyle pointed out a number of what he called "foundation features" that were identical. And the shape of the skulls merged perfectly.

"Impressive," I said.

"But wait," he said with a grin, "there's more. Remember I told you I had lifted Amanda Miller's fingerprints? Amy couldn't find a match in any of the databases she could get into."

"Doesn't the DMV have thumbprints?"

"They do, but Amy says she can't hack into the California DMV database. The security is too good and it really pisses her off. She used to have a DMV contact that would run stuff for her, but not anymore."

"So?"

"So I got lucky. I was talking to your IT guy about the prints and all, and he got a funny look on his face. You know that new feature in MySlice pizzerias where they identify you by your thumb print on an iPad? Well, it seems that just before she left, they were testing it on a bunch of the admins. That included Tracy.

"Now, you don't store the print itself. It gets translated to a series of numbers. No two prints generate the same numbers. It's those numbers that go in the database. For security, it's a one-way algorithm. You can't reconstruct a print from those numbers. But if the numbers match, they came from the same thumb."

"And you had Amanda Miller's thumb print."

"I did," he said smugly. "From the same hand."

"And the magic numbers match," I said.

"Yes, they do."

"Now what happens?"

"We want to get back the money she and Angie Grey stole from Zack's foundation. Amy and I have cooked up a plan to do that. But we need your help."

Vito Cangelosi was the uncle of my best childhood friend, Nick Marchetti. When we were kids growing up on Long Island, Nick and I spent a lot of time at the Marchetti house, and I was pretty much an honorary member of the family. Uncle Vito was this big, gruff-voiced, kind, generous guy who visited frequently, and played Santa Claus to all the kids in Nick's neighborhood each Christmas.

He had also been a mobster and official in the New York City longshoreman's union. Now he lived in a well-guarded compound near Phoenix that was surrounded by a ten-foot high fence topped with razor wire. Large hungry dogs roamed the grounds. From his desert fortress, Uncle Vito ran a limousine service staffed mostly by other "retired" wiseguys, happy to have put 2,400 miles between themselves and the New York docks.

Uncle Vito was certain the Feds were tapping his phones. So talking to him required following a certain ritual.

"Tan Limousine Service," a cheerful voice announced. "How can I help you?"

"I'd like to arrange some transportation using your platinum service," I said. "Platinum service" was code for "give this message to the boss." Uncle Vito loved codes.

"And who will we be transporting?"

"Mike Gold."

"I'm going to put you on hold for a moment, Mr. Gold."

She was quickly back on the line. "Thank you for holding. I apologize for the delay. To finalize your arrangements, I am texting you a number."

We disconnected. My phone announced that it had received a new text message. I called the number in the text.

"Ah, Michael. This, ah, secure phone takes a while to scramble or whatever the hell it does."

I had tried a number of times to explain to Uncle Vito that secure phone calls require the same type of encryption technology at both ends. But he firmly believed his calls were secure, and I eventually gave up trying to convince him otherwise.

His voice was softer than I expected. I thought that maybe it was due to his phone security software doing whatever useless stuff it does. "How are you, Uncle Vito?"

"Getting too old, Michael. What about you and Lisa? Heard you had some excitement."

I caught him up on our recent adventures. He hadn't heard about Brian, so we spent some time chatting about my being a grandpa.

"Okay, kid, whadaya need?" Uncle Vito was no one's fool and, when he got down to business, you had better do so as well.

I explained. He listened in silence until I finished.

"So this was your idea or Kyle's?" he said.

Kyle Rizzo was the grandson of one of Uncle Vito's limo drivers, a trim, dapper guy named Eddie. It was through Uncle Vito that I had first met Kyle way back when. Through some intricate family relationships I could never follow, they were related, and Kyle called Vito uncle. Then again, so did I.

"Mostly Kyle's," I said.

"Whodda thought Eddie would have such a bright grandson?"

Uncle Vito said that if I could get the FBI to go along, he'd do his part. He said he really wanted to see his nephew Nick again before he died.

Two days later, Alex Greene and I met for lunch at the Los Gatos MySlice. After the hubbub over having the CEO show up had died down, we were left alone to munch our pizza.

"Nice to see they're so excited to see an FBI agent," he said.

"Not just any FBI agent," I said. "A special agent in charge."

"I wonder how they knew?"

"Your SliceBank account knows all," I said. Actually, that was not at all true. We mainly knew about his pizza preferences.

"How is Lisa?"

"She's good. Her doctor cleared her to drive yesterday. I had to insist she also ask him about flying her plane. The doc suggested she wait another week, just to be on the safe side. But her main issue is her hair. Some of it was shaved off so they could treat the bullet wound."

"I know all about the hair," he said.

We nodded at each other. Male bonding over female idiosyncrasies.

"And how are you, Mike?"

"Avoiding men dressed like Darth Vader with bombs taped to their chests," I said.

"Words to live by," he said.

I gave Alex a quick summary of my physical condition. I had great progress to report. I did not discuss my mental condition, where the progress was more ambiguous.

"So what's up?"

"You think it isn't just your company I seek?" I said.

I had never seen an FBI agent roll his eyes before. It was quite a sight. I thought that Will Smith, Greene's doppelganger, could not have pulled it off half as well.

"This has a bit to do with Nick Marchetti. So let me be clear, I've had no contact with Nick since he disappeared seven years ago. And I don't know how to contact him. I'm an intermediary."

"Who for?"

"I won't say. That's not negotiable."

He thought a bit, then sighed. "Okay, go ahead."

I told him the Tracy Luce-Amanda Miller story. He listened attentively. He asked few questions, but those he did ask were right on point.

Then I told him what we wanted to do, and what I needed from him. I did not mention Uncle Vito's role. I was vague about how we'd get the money back, and how we knew what we knew in the first place. But I let Greene read between the lines.

When I finished, he was silent for a while. I waited patiently. I was asking for a lot of trust from an agency that trusts no one. Still, Greene and I had a history, and I believed I had earned his trust.

"You don't ask for much, do you, Mr. Gold?"

When Alex Greene was switching into full FBI mode, I became Mr. Gold.

"I think it's a fair trade," I said. "You get Tracy Luce for embezzlement. You get to take credit for recovering the foundations money. Besides, you guys must have given up on Nick by now. You didn't have much on him in the first place."

Nick Marchetti was the financial genius behind Forward Data Systems. He'd helped make its founder and CEO Barry Samson one of the 10 richest men in the world. Then they had a falling out and Nick left to form his very successful venture capital firm.

When he was in college, Nick had fathered a daughter. She knew nothing about him, though he helped support her and watched her from a distance. Then in her twenties, Samson started dating her. Nick knew how Samson had treated the string of twenty-something women he had gone through over the years. He used them, abused them, and then discarded them like unwanted trash. Most were left with deep emotional scars.

Nick asked Samson to leave his daughter alone. Samson laughed in his face. Shortly thereafter, Samson was murdered by his chauffeur and bodyguard, Buck Peters. Peters was the brother of Nick's girlfriend, Rhonda Jackson.

The Samson murder attracted immense law enforcement attention. The evidence against Peters was conclusive, but he vanished, as did Nick and Rhonda. That was about seven years ago. The Feds had been looking for the three fugitives ever since.

"We know Buck Peters murdered Barry Samson," Greene said.

I nodded.

"We know Peters was Rhonda Jackson's brother, and she was Marchetti's girlfriend.

I nodded again. What they didn't know was that Samson's girlfriend was Nick's daughter.

"We know that there was no love lost between Samson and Marchetti."

"If every sour business relationship in the valley led to murder, we'd still have orchards everywhere," I said.

"And Marchetti and Jackson disappeared, along with his yacht, just about the same time Peters fled to Mexico."

"What you have are coincidences. You have no evidence that Nick or Rhonda were involved in Samson's murder. You have no evidence that they helped Peters escape. In fact, you have a confession by a mobster that he was the one who was in cahoots with Peters." That last item was thanks to Uncle Vito. He got one of his men who was dying of cancer to make up a confession. The guy then clammed up and died in jail.

"Without Marchetti, we got no motive," Greene said, though I sensed he was weakening.

"So catch Peters and ask him. He worked as Samson's chauffeur and bodyguard. Samson was a prick. There could have been any number of personal motives. Hell, Alex, you even thought I was involved in some sort of conspiracy to kill Samson." At the time of the murder, I was running a little company doing business with Samson and Nick. For a while, Greene, then a mere special agent, was making a circumstantial case against me. The confession Uncle Vito arranged put a quick end to that; Uncle Vito did it for me.

"You were connected to all the players," Greene said. "You had a financial motive."

"And the Feds were desperate for an arrest."

"There may have been some pressure coming down..."

"Look, Alex, we're giving you a woman who embezzled 50 million dollars from a charitable foundation. You'll bask in the glory of recovering the money. In exchange, you drop the bogus warrants against Nick and Rhonda. Let them come home and leave them alone."

"How is it you keep giving me these career enhancing opportunities?" he said.

This was not the first time I had given Greene leads that had increased his stature in the FBI. In fact, he had once admitted that I was instrumental in getting him promoted over others to special agent in charge.

"I'm just a good citizen who stumbles across evildoers," I said. 'Then I do my civic duty."

"You know I'm going to have to run this upstairs," he said.

"Then run," I said. "Fast. She could take off at any time."

Chapter 9

Lisa called the hospital again. Once more, she was told that Sam Jones's condition was stable. No, they could not tell her anything more. It was a privacy thing, which she supposed made sense. No, he could not have a visitor. No, he was not to have any phone calls. Except for immediate family. Which she wasn't.

That really puzzled Lisa. A few days after running its lengthy story on Giuseppe Brandetti, the Mercury-News had run a similarly long article about Sam Jones. Jones had arrived in Silicon Valley about 10 years ago. He'd worked as an angel investor, providing seed money to erstwhile tech entrepreneurs to help them get their companies started. The reporter had interviewed a few of the people he'd worked with and they'd said nice things about him.

Jones lived alone in an upscale neighborhood in Los Gatos, about a mile from Lisa and Mike's place. Neighbors described him as a nice guy who was out puttering in his yard most weekends and always had a friendly hello for them. He was known to the neighborhood kids as a guy who was good at fixing bikes and skateboards.

Nice was the word that seemed to describe Sam Jones.

Lisa noted that there was no mention of a girlfriend or boyfriend, or any family. The reporter quoted his next door neighbor, who said that Jones had told her he was an orphan and had grown up in foster homes somewhere back East.

Ted Trotter had also run a piece on CNN about Sam Jones. It more or less summarized the Mercury-News article. Trotter finished the story with his usual teaser. "We still don't know why Giuseppe Brandetti tried to murder Sam Jones," he intoned dramatically. "What are the authorities hiding?"

Lisa thought that the authorities didn't want to say the obvious: Brandetti was a narcissistic hothead who was at the end of his rope and finally snapped when he realized the world was not going to work his way.

Lisa was frustrated. She just wanted to talk to Jones and see how he was doing. She'd been told that only family could call or visit, but there didn't seem to be any family.

The other thing on Lisa's mind was that the tiger dream was back.

As a little girl, Lisa had a recurring nightmare: there was a tiger under her bed and it was waiting to pounce on her. Sometimes it had roared and jarred her awake, terrified.

As she got older, the nightmare came less frequently. Until about a year ago, she hadn't had it at all since she met Mike. Or, she thought, she didn't remember having it. Lisa rarely remembered a dream, unlike her husband, who seemed to recall at least one dream every night, often in rich detail.

She had realized she was having the tiger dream again a year or so ago, not long after the Woodchipper Incident. Lisa had been kidnapped in an attempt to lure Mike to a deserted cabin in the Santa Cruz Mountains. The kidnappers planned to then put Lisa and Mike through a woodchipper. With Kyle Rizzo's help, they were rescued, but the psychic scar of that terror had run deep for both of them.

They had been in Maui, recovering from that experience with the help of a great psychotherapist, when Mike was asked to become CEO of MySlice after Zack Zander's murder. She thought they had both healed their shattered psyches. The dream had stopped, and they had come home.

But right after she'd been shot, the tiger had returned.

Chapter 10

The day after he saw the bastard on TV, Baxter had called in sick at his crappy night watchman job in Gary, Indiana, and headed west for Napa, California. Hightower may have shaved his head and grown a beard, but Baxter was certain he and Jones were one in the same. Every detail of Hightower's face was obsessively etched in his mind.

Like Lisa, he got the same stonewall when he called the hospital about seeing Sam Jones. But that didn't stop him.

Baxter figured you could go pretty much anywhere in a hospital if you were wheeling an old person in a wheelchair. It was easy to rent the wheelchair, but there wasn't exactly a rent-a-geezer service he could use.

He solved that problem when he saw a sign for the Veterans Home in Yountville. He drove over and, sure enough, there were a number of elderly vets sitting on benches feeding the birds. After a little schmoozing, he found eighty-something Wayne. Bored and aching for a little adventure, Wayne readily agreed to play a part in Baxter's little charade. They agreed on fifteen dollars an hour, cash.

He picked Wayne up the next morning. Wayne provided his own costume: faded blue and white pajamas and a pair of well-worn slippers. He hadn't shaved, and his gray stubble, thinning grey hair and sagging wattle completed the doddering old-man effect.

Baxter started getting smiles from people as soon as he began wheeling gaunt old Wayne through the hospital parking lot. The slight hitch in Baxter's gait, the result of an injury during a dustup in military prison, made him an even more sympathetic figure. He could imagine their thoughts: *Such a nice man. He's taking his grandpa in for treatment.*

He already knew Jones's room number. The day before, he had presented himself at the hospital information desk. He was carrying a bouquet of flowers and a clipboard. Consulting the clipboard, he told the elderly woman at the desk that he had flowers to deliver to a Mr. Sam Jones. After a moment fiddling with her computer, she told him that Mr. Jones was not receiving visitors. He explained he was not a visitor, just a delivery man.

The helpful lady was flummoxed. She didn't have any information in her computer about deliveries for Mr. Jones. She thought about taking the flowers, but then how would she get them up to his room?

Ever helpful, Baxter suggested that he drop the flowers at the nursing station. The relieved helpful lady jumped at this, and gave him directions.

Baxter had timed his arrival for afternoon shift change. When he got to the nursing station, several nurses going off-duty were hurriedly exchanging information with their relief. He politely interrupted one such pair, and, checking his clipboard for the name, asked if he could deliver the flowers he held to Mr. Jones. The anxious-to-leave nurse brusquely told him the room number and said to leave the flowers with the guard at the door.

Baxter walked in the direction of the room, past the seated, bored looking deputy who did not even look up from his magazine, and through the door at the end of the hall. Moments later, he had gone down the stairs and out of the hospital. Baxter now knew Jones's room number. He also knew the room was guarded.

Baxter slowly, casually wheeled Wayne down the hall, past Jones's room. Just taking the old guy for a walk. He did a U-turn at the end of the hall. When they neared Jones's room, Wayne loudly told him to stop.

"What are you up to, sonny?" He shouted at the seated deputy.

"Keep your voice down, Grandpa," Baxter said. To the deputy, he said, "I'm sorry, his hearing is pretty much gone. He won't wear a hearing aid, so he shouts a lot and yells at people to speak up."

The guard appeared eager to have something to do to break the monotony. "My grandfather's the same way," he said, shaking his head to indicate his understanding of Baxter's plight.

"Who you got in there? Some kinda crook? Wha'd he do?" Wayne was grinning broadly and still shouting.

"Grandpa, please, let's go."

"I don't wanna go!"

"What's your name, sir?"

Wayne lowered his volume a bit. "Name's Wayne. Korean War. You?"

"Afghanistan." The deputy quickly added, "That was before I joined the sheriff's department."

Baxter and Wayne were back in his car.

"You get a good look at him when that nurse went in?" Wayne said.

"I did. It's him alright. But I was careful not to let him see me. Tell me, how'd you know to ask that guard about his service?"

"Something about the way he called me sir, his haircut, hell, he just looked like a G.I. Figured it was worth a shot."

"You are a clever old goat, aren't you?"

"More'n you know. And I don't believe he's a sheriff's deputy, do you?"

"Yeah, I thought he was trying to cover up his blunder."

"So your boy's being guarded by the military," said Wayne. "What's next?"

Baxter decided Wayne had earned a nice lunch before he took him back to the Veterans Home. As for what to do next, he'd need some time to think about that.

Chapter 11

The *Harbor Rat* did not go unnoticed as it slipped into Tulula harbor.

Once just a sleepy fishing village, Tulula had become a secluded stopover for yachts travelling among the tiny Polynesian islands in this remote region of the South Pacific. Even for Samoa, Tulula was isolated. Most who came in their sleek, expensive boats were seeking utmost privacy. These visitors were few and far between, but they were always a target of curiosity and a source of income for Tulula's residents.

A decade before, Rick Manville, Tulula's most notorious and wealthiest businessman, had expanded the fishing docks and built up the local marina to be able to moor and service his schooner and the yachts of others with wealth and a penchant for discreet luxury.

Most of the many Manville legends centered on Wall Street shenanigans that had brought him to Samoa at the start of the Great Recession. Conveniently, Samoa did not have an extradition treaty with the United States.

Soon the Manville Development Company had transformed the shanty downtown by the addition of tasteful small shops and restaurants that catered to the needs of Manville Marina's very upscale guests. Manville Estates, a gated community of villas, grew where before there had been only jungle that sloped gently upward from Main Street, which had been the village's only paved road. All the villas had verandas with spectacular views of the harbor and beaches across that Main Street, and the glorious blue-green ocean beyond.

The global economic collapse turned out to be a boon for Manville Enterprises. As Samoa's two main trading partners, Australia and New Zealand, dove into recession, Samoa had followed, and then some. Manville found suppliers and contractors falling over each other bidding for his construction business. Best of all, his expensive but oh-so-private marina and residential units were just the thing for financial renegades with millions in hot cash to spend in a country that did not extradite.

The locals who staffed the shops and marina, and serviced the villas, continued to live in the same huts and bungalows as before the new development, but they now had internet and cell phone service, indoor plumbing, and newer cars and scooters parked in the carports.

A man they were to learn was the *Harbor Rat's* captain came ashore in a small outboard. After he made the necessary arrangements with the dock master, he stopped at the local government office. This two desk storefront housed the village policeman and an all-purpose government clerk. Together, they represented the Samoan government in the capital city of Apia.

It was assumed that money changed hands. The policeman left the office and soon returned, accompanied by two local sometime-dockhands, Isaac and Tupa. They joined the captain and the policeman in animated conversation, then the two rugged men left with the captain and followed him aboard the *Harbor Rat*.

A short time later, Isaac left and went directly to the combination general store and bar and grill where the locals tended to congregate. Instantly the center of undivided attention and a continuous supply of his favorite beer, he revealed that they had been hired to provide twenty-four by seven security, working twelve-hour shifts. Isaac would work the night shift.

The *Harbor Rat* had four occupants, he told the eager crowd. The captain, Diego, was perhaps sixty years old, a squat, weathered Hispanic who spoke English with a heavy Mexican accent. He had one deckhand named Bubba, a tall, muscular black man in his thirties. Their passengers were a man and woman, obviously a couple.

The man, Vic, appeared to be in his forties. He was Caucasian, dark, slim, just under six feet tall, with a full head of black hair and deep brown eyes. It was said that he had a cold, hard, penetrating stare. He spoke American English like a native.

The woman, Brenda, was black and stately, a bit taller than the man, and most attractive. The consensus was that she was in her thirties. She too spoke perfect American English, but also Samoan, though with an American accent. It was highly unusual for a foreigner who was not of Samoan ancestry—and she certainly did not look Samoan—to speak the native language.

Isaac concluded his report with two more tidbits. No last names had been offered, and the newcomers would be living on the yacht, not renting a villa.

The village was intrigued.

Brenda, Vic and Bubba came ashore every day in the early morning, when it was as cool as it gets in the tropics. They would jog for half an hour, then promptly return to the yacht.

Later each day, Brenda and Vic would again come ashore, sometimes for lunch, sometimes for dinner. The couple sampled each of Tulula's restaurants, even those that catered to the locals. They occasionally browsed the shops but purchased little. They were polite but reserved.

Occasionally, Captain Diego and Bubba would come ashore for supplies. They were businesslike and did not linger on shore or mix with the locals.

All four paid only in cash, which was not unusual for the marina's guests. A yacht such as *Harbor Rat* always had a sturdy safe. Still, this further explained the security guards.

Word of the newcomers reached Amanda Miller the evening of the day the *Harbor Rat* arrived. She received a complete account from her live-in housekeeper and lover, Sefina, Isaac's cousin. Sefina had been in the general store when Isaac told his tale, and got some extra juicy details from him when he helped her take the groceries back to Amanda's villa.

Amanda found slender young Sefina irresistible, and so tolerated her mindless chatter. Thus she paid little attention to the gossip.

But two weeks later, she found herself pumping Sefina for every bit of information she had on Brenda and Vic. Vic had called her that morning. He was interested in perhaps purchasing a home in Manville Estates. An appointment for the following day was made.

Amanda Miller had arrived in Tulula less than a year ago. She had been referred to Rick Manville by her banker in the Cook Islands, the banking haven a thousand miles southeast of Samoa, half way to Tahiti. Amanda's problem was that she had 50 million embezzled American dollars safely tucked away in her Cook Island bank, but it was difficult to get access to the money and still keep it hidden. A classic problem, her banker explained. The solution was to find a way to launder the funds. He often helped clients with such difficulties. Rick Manville had been one such client.

The ever helpful banker had helped Manville establish Manville Enterprises in Samoa with capital supplied by an investment company in the Cook Islands. The investment company had been set up by a local lawyer, whose name was the only one that appeared on any documents associated with it. The funds from Manville's Cook Island account were transferred to the investment company, then to the Manville Enterprises account, and just like that, they had been cleansed.

Now, he told Amanda, Manville Enterprises consisted of Manville Marina, Manville Development Company, and

Manville Property Management. The development company had built the marina, the new stores in town, and Manville Estates. Manville Marina owned and operated the marina. The property management company rented and maintained the stores and serviced their tenants. It also handled sales and rentals of villas—some were privately owned, some were rentals—and serviced and maintained those properties.

Rick Manville and Amanda Miller quickly struck a deal. Amanda invested 45 million dollars in Manville Enterprises. She also became head of Manville Property Management. And thus it was she who would attempt to sell a villa to the mysterious Brenda and Vic.

Chapter 12

The showing went well enough. Brenda and Vic seemed impressed with the spacious rooms, infinity pools and high-end appliances the Manville villas featured. There were three basic models, though they could be customized as much as the client wished—at an appropriate cost.

Brenda seemed ready to buy. She said things to Vic about finally having a place to stay instead of travelling around all the time. She was tired of the yachting life. She favored the most expensive of the models, and Amanda thought she would be happy to purchase the one she'd shown them that was vacant and occasionally used as a rental.

Vic would be the tough nut. He intimidated her. When they spoke to each other, he locked his eyes onto hers with a discomfiting intensity. If she were into men, she felt she would be quite vulnerable to the power of this focus, as if the two of them were alone in the universe.

He seemed happy enough with the houses and the property. He asked a lot of questions about security and maintenance, and appeared to be pleased with her answers. But as the showing wound down, he seemed anxious to leave. Price had yet to be discussed, and even for the rich that was not a good sign.

Two days later, hearing nothing, Amanda called Vic and asked if she could be of further service. Did the couple need any more information?

Vic politely declined her offer. He said they would get back to her.

Two more days passed. Then Brenda called. Would Amanda join them for an outing on the yacht? Perhaps they could discuss the villas in a more casual setting. The subtext was that she and Amanda might be able to soften Vic up after a few hours of wine, sun and salt air.

The next day, Diego guided Amanda, Brenda and Vic out of the harbor. Bubba had chosen to stay on shore.

It is remarkable how quickly you can lose sight of land when boating among the tiny islands in the vast South Pacific. Equally remarkable is the seemingly infinite sameness of those waters with no land for points of reference. As the day lazily wore on, the *Harbor Rat* drifted slowly eastward.

In 1899, Great Britain, Germany and the United States ended a series of clashes among them for control over the Samoan Islands. Germany got control over present-day and now independent Samoa, west of 171 degrees longitude. The islands to the east of that line became American Samoa, a U.S. territory. Britain got control of other territories elsewhere. Less than 40 miles separates Tulula in Samoa from American Samoan waters.

The ocean did not care about the 171 degrees longitude line of demarcation; nothing was etched on its azure surface to mark it.

Amanda thought the day was going splendidly. Vic had taught her how to fish, and she'd actually landed a small tuna. Wine flowed, along with an assortment of tasty treats to nibble. Vic seemed to be responding to her subtle flirting and flattery, and Brenda had whispered to her that he "seemed to be coming around."

The fierce looking, fast-moving grey boat with U. S. Coast Guard emblazoned on the side seemed to come out of nowhere. As it slowed next to the *Harbor Rat,* a voice on a bullhorn boomed, *"Harbor Rat*, cut your engines and prepare to be boarded."

In moments, the two boats were held side-by-side by rope lines. Two sharp looking young sailors hopped aboard smoothly. Then they helped a serious looking woman in civilian dress cross the gap between the vessels. The woman took a moment to steady herself, then took what appeared to be 8x10 photos out of a slim portfolio and looked back-and-forth between the pictures and Amanda, Brenda and Vic.

"I'm FBI. Special Agent Loni Davis. Tracy Luce, Rhonda Jackson, Nicholas Marchetti, I am placing you under arrest. You have the right to remain silent..."

Tracy felt herself go numb. *This cannot be happening. Rhonda Jackson? Nicholas Marchetti? What the fuck!*

The three were flexicuffed and helped aboard the Coast Guard cutter. "My name is Amanda Miller," Tracy screamed at the FBI agent. "You have no jurisdiction in Samoa."

"That's true, ma'am, but you crossed into American Samoan waters about a half hour ago. Welcome to the United States of America."

"I demand to see a lawyer. Where are you taking us?"

"You'll get to see your lawyer as soon you're processed into the system. That will happen as soon as we get to Hawaii. We fly out in two hours."

Only much later did it occur to Tracy that her two companions had been oddly silent and relaxed during what she viewed as a terrifying nightmare.

Diego guided the *Harbor Rat* to its rendezvous with its launch in a secluded cove some distance from Tulula harbor. After they secured the launch onboard, Diego and Bubba, whose real name was Buck Peters, headed out into the open ocean. They would scrupulously avoid American Samoan waters.

The next morning, as Rick Manville was worrying about Amanda and contemplating organizing a search for the missing *Harbor Rat*, his secretary informed him that two men were asking to see him. They would not, she said, reveal their names or business with Mr. Manville.

What the hell? He thought. *I might as well see them and get it over with.*

The men his secretary showed in seemed to fill Rick's office. It wasn't so much their size, though they were tall, barrel-chested, and the upper arms of their suit coats bulged. No, it was more the menace they exuded that fairly filled the room.

As he sized them up, Rick thought how odd it was to see men in dark suits, white shirts, neckties and dress shoes in Tulula. More, they seemed not to be affected by the steamy climate. Even with the air conditioning at full blast, Rick was mildly uncomfortable in his open-necked, short-sleeved shirt, shorts and sandals. These two looked cool, calm and dry.

"How can I help you, gentlemen?"

The one on the left did all the talking. As soon as he began, Nick's stomach lurched. The Brooklyn accent, the deliberately soft voice, the artificial politeness, propelled him back to his years in New York. He'd dealt with these wiseguys before. No, not these two exactly, but their clones. The New York mob seemed to have an unlimited supply of them.

An hour later, the men left. If he did as he was told, they would not return. If not, well, that would be "the biggest mistake of your life." He had 48 hours.

As he downed a large pour of scotch, Rick Manville thought wryly that they had indeed made him an offer he couldn't refuse.

Chapter 13

When the thugs left, Rick Manville took a couple of stiff drinks and reflected on how he'd gotten into this shit.

He was a survivor. He was born Richard Van Mille in a dirt-poor section of Brooklyn. His mother named him after her best guess as to the name of the long-gone man she thought might have been his father. She wasn't really sure about how he had pronounced his name, never mind how it was spelled.

Scrappy Ricky managed to survive the mean streets and scraped his way through City College. He supported himself through school by working as a runner for the Brooklyn mob. A runner was a glorified errand boy, as in, "hey kid, run over to ... and ..."

He graduated from college just as the subprime mortgage bubble got started. A glib kid, he found work in a mortgage office selling home loans to the working poor. He was a master at forging documentation. His clients never read the documents he asked them to sign. They could in fact manage, often barely, to eke out the payments at the teaser rates, and it would be years before the mortgages reset to a hopelessly unaffordable level. Meanwhile, they thought they could afford the American dream, a home of their own.

After a few months, Ricky saw that this could be a gold mine. He managed to get the ear of one of the mob bosses he'd run errands for. He agreed to back Ricky's idea.

Soon, Ricky Van Mille oversaw a chain of store front mortgage mills located in poor neighborhoods throughout the metropolitan New York area. The formula was simple. Originate the mortgage, backed by mob money. Instantly sell the mortgage to one of the many banks who were falling all over each other to bundle large batches of subprime loans together and "securitize" them. Then, poof! High risk mortgages were magically transformed into ostensibly low risk, high yield securities, foisted on hoodwinked investors.

Van Mille made money for himself and his backers through generous fees paid by the ravenous banks for originating and selling them the loans. He also laundered vast sums of illicit mob money by initially funding the mortgages. That money was returned, properly laundered, when each mortgage was resold.

Ricky had one other innovation. He put mob soldiers on the payroll. These wiseguys never showed up for work but received paychecks directly deposited regardless. Thus he paid his mob bosses their profits by paying their troops.

It took several years before the subprime bubble burst. When it did, Ricky Van Mille was left holding the bag. He was indicted for fraud, racketeering, and a host of other transgressions. He had stashed much of his personal hoard in the Cook Islands, and when the axe fell, he fairly sprinted to Samoa, the land of no extradition.

So when the two old thugs showed up in his office, he understood their message. They knew who he was. The talker mentioned the right names. He knew the drill: shut up and listen.

The mob had left him alone after he'd fled to Samoa. He had made them a ton of money and kept up his end of the bargain: he took the fall. He'd changed his name around— he actually liked the manly sound of Rick Manville a lot better than Ricky Van Mille—but he wasn't trying too hard to hide out. The mob wasn't after him, and the Feds couldn't get to him because he was in the paradise of non-extradition.

Now, as the talker had said, Rick had "inadvertently stepped in it." He sighed, went to the window, and looked out over the marina. Time to bite the bullet. It wouldn't take him the 48 hours they'd given him to follow their instructions. It took just one phone call. That same day, as he'd been directed, 45 million dollars was wired from Manville Enterprises to the Zack Zander Foundation.

Rick Manville had purchased friends in high places in Samoa. He filed a lawsuit that day in Samoa's capital, Apia, charging Amanda Miller with fraud and breach of contract. While Amanda Miller was being transferred in FBI custody from American Samoa to Hawaii, Manville was seeing to it that her bank account containing over four million dollars was frozen. It would take but a few weeks for him to win a default judgement against her. He was awarded all of her

Samoan assets, mainly that bank account. Their partnership was declared null and void.

The thugs never returned. Rick Manville figured he had come out way ahead. He had made a tidy profit and was still breathing.

Chapter 14

"Nick's on his way home!"

I was jumping out of my skin. All I wanted to do was hug Lisa, but she was up at the winery for a few days, and I was in New York making the rounds of Wall Street financial analysts. So I had to settle for a phone call. She had been in a particularly good mood of late. She was flying her Cessna again. She was working full tilt again. She got to see her grandson regularly. And her hair was growing back nicely.

"That's great news!" she said. "When?"

"A couple of days. The plan worked perfectly. Nick and Rhonda are in Hawaii. Annie flew out to be sure the legal stuff is done just right."

"I'll be home tomorrow," she said. "We can start planning how to celebrate."

"I'll be flying out of here around noon, so I won't be home until late," I said. "Don't forget the time zone difference."

"I'll keep the bed warm for you," Lisa said.

When I'd first told Lisa about Kyle's plan, she'd looked at me with that elevating eyebrow of hers. "Do you want to get into this sort of thing again?"

When Lisa says, "Do you want..." to me, it's rarely really a question. What she usually means is either, "I want you to..." as in, "Do you want to take out the garbage?" or, "I don't want you to..." as in, "Do you want to wear that tie?" I knew in this case she meant the latter.

But I'd chosen to pretend it was really a question, as I sometimes stubbornly do even after years of training. And it was a good question. The Halloween Explosion had left me emotionally shattered. I'd had a lot of psychotherapy from a very good therapist over the intervening months. My inner Spock was now in pretty good shape. Ever logical, he knew the mistake I had made was trying to play god and set the world right all by myself. I somehow wanted to right the wrongs of the Fed Deal without harming MySlice. So I'd decided to administer my own brand of justice. For my inner Spock, it was a lesson learned.

My inner Kirk was another story. Impulsive though he was, he still did not understand why I had acted so rashly, causing Doyle's and Harper's deaths, and very nearly my own. He still had, as the shrinks like to say, a lot of unresolved issues.

At our last session in Napa, my therapist said something that stayed with me. "Never forget that Spock and Kirk are just useful ways of thinking about the logical and emotional parts of you. Those parts need to be integrated, not separated."

But I felt I had reached an impasse in my psychotherapy. My therapist preferred to call it a plateau. Regardless, we had agreed that I would take a break.

I had told Lisa that, yes, I did want to do my part in the plan, but just my small part. This wasn't my plan, it was Kyle's. She had agreed, grudgingly at first, but soon warmed up to the scheme. I think conning the bad guys especially appealed to her. And she did want to have Nick back home.

After he returned from his scouting trip to Samoa, in addition to searching for information about Amanda Miller, Kyle and Amy tried to get background on Rick Manville. Kyle had a photo he'd taken and some information about Manville's activities since he'd arrived at Samoa. They found information online for several Rick or Richard Manvilles, but none that fit. They concluded that Rick Manville was probably an alias.

On a whim, Kyle had asked his Uncle Vito if he had ever heard of a guy named Rick Manville. He hadn't, but the next day, Uncle Vito called back. The name had struck a familiar chord with wily old Vito Cangelosi, and a bit later the name Ricky Van Mille suddenly popped into his head. Van Mille's mortgage deal had gotten going strong about the time Uncle Vito had retreated to the desert.

That was all Kyle and Amy needed. Moments after googling Ricky Van Mille they had a load of information. More, Kyle had gotten an idea about how he could use Manville's mob connection to get the foundation's money back, bring the embezzler to justice, and bring his cousin Nick home.

My role was twofold. First, I had to get the Feds to drop all charges against Nick and Rhonda, which was why I had met with Greene. In exchange, the FBI would get the Zack Zander Foundation embezzler and take credit for recovering most of the money.

My second job was to explain the plan to Uncle Vito. Kyle felt it would have a lot more credibility with the old man coming from me than from him. Uncle Vito had readily agreed. He wanted his favorite nephew Nick home before he died. He knew how to contact him. He would explain to Nick how the con needed to be run.

The end game of the con was simple: get Tracy Luce, alias Amanda Miller, into American Samoan waters so the Feds could take her into custody. To preserve their cover, the Feds would take Rhonda and Nick into custody as well. While the end game was unfolding, Buck Peters, still wanted in the U.S. for murder, would remain in Samoa, out of reach of American authorities.

Uncle Vito would also dispatch two of Tan Limousine Service's most intimidating looking employees to Samoa. They would wait for a call from Diego that Luce had been taken into custody. Then they would pay Rick Manville a little visit, imply they'd been sent by the New York mob, and tell him that he had to return Amanda's money to the Zack Zander Foundation.

I had only given Greene the broad outline of the plan. The Feds didn't need to know the details, especially about Uncle Vito. If we failed to deliver, if somehow the Tracy Luce/ Amanda Miller thing didn't pan out, they'd still have Nick and Rhonda in custody.

It all fell into place when Greene got the okay from his boss. He told me it had gone all the way to the Director of the FBI and the Attorney General. The Director was fine with the trade, but at first the A.G. balked. Then—and here Greene reminded me we were completely off the record and he'd deny ever saying it—the Director reminded the A.G. that Mike Gold had some juice with the President.

Which was true. A few years ago, I had done something at the President's behest that helped with the cleanup of the Deepwater Horizon oil spill in the Gulf of Mexico. The White House emissary had specifically called what I did a favor. About the same time, I had gotten into some legal trouble—I was arrested for murder—and it seems the President had heard about the situation and asked the A.G. and FBI Director to keep an eye on it. The charges were soon dropped. I don't think anyone had intervened on my behalf, but I was now hearing that it pays to do the President of the United States a favor. As my grandma would have said, "It wouldn't hurt!"

With the Feds onboard, Annie Oakley and a government attorney fussed over the actual legal agreement. Part of that was our insistence that Nick and Rhonda be kept out of the Tracy Luce prosecution. Once they had Luce in custody, the FBI could match her prints to the California DMV database for a positive ID, so there would be no connection to MySlice or me. With Amy's information, they could easily trace the money from Zack's Foundation to Manville Enterprises. And Greene had assured me they could develop plenty of evidence to nail Luce on the embezzlement. "That's what the FBI does best, Mike.

Investigation. It's part of our name." They wouldn't need any testimony from Nick or Rhonda.

With the lawyers done, the wheels of this peculiar adventure in justice started to turn. Nick and his crew headed to Tulula, Samoa in the *Harbor Rat* from somewhere in the South Pacific—I later learned it was Tahiti. And so the games began.

Chapter 15

Nick Marchetti's return to Silicon Valley did not go unnoticed. He had been one of the Valley's most prominent venture capitalists and had disappeared under a cloud of suspicion about involvement in Barry Samson's murder. He decided to head that off by holding a press conference. Better to shape the news himself than let speculation do it.

I drove up to the San Jose Fairmont and was greeted warmly by the doorman, Oliver. As usual, I over-tipped him, knowing he would keep my Lexus under the front portico instead of in the bowels of the parking garage.

The press conference was in a small meeting room on the second floor of this fine hotel. Nick and Rhonda stood side-by-side behind a lectern with a forest of microphones in front of it. Annie Oakley stood off to the side behind them, poised to spring if her lawyerly services became necessary. There were about twenty people sitting on folding chairs in the audience besides me. I sat in the last row. I recognized several business news reporters who covered Silicon Valley.

Nick tapped the mike. "I have a brief statement to read, then we'll take a few questions.

"Rhonda and I have been on an extended yachting trip around the world. Part of the reason for the trip was to get away from the unwanted attention we were getting about Barry Samson's death. We recently decided it was time to come home. We met with the FBI in Hawaii, and were assured that we were no longer persons of interest in that case.

"The FBI also told us that Rhonda's brother, Buck Peters, remains the prime suspect in Samson's murder. We told them the truth, that we do not know his whereabouts.

"Now we are going to spend some time visiting with friends and family and then we'll decide what to do with the rest of our lives.

"Okay, we'll be glad to take your questions."

Sort of glad. Nick refused to say anything further about Buck or Samson's murder. So they directed a similar question to Rhonda, who also politely stonewalled. It's hard to make news out of "no comment." They both shaped their answers to the Q&A to deliver one message: Nick Marchetti was a rich guy who had enjoyed yachting around the world for seven years with his beautiful girlfriend. And she'd enjoyed it too.

As I slipped out the door at the rear of the room, I caught Nick's eye. I winked. He smiled an acknowledgement. *Well done, Nick.*

Nick and I were sitting in our family room. Lisa and Rhonda were in the kitchen doing something `or other women do after dinner. It seemed to mainly involve talking and laughing.

Rhonda and Nick had insisted on a simple, intimate welcome back celebration—dinner at our house, just the four of us, would be perfect, they said. They were really just stopping over on their way to New York, where they would spend a week or so with Nick's very large family. Then they planned to spend a few days in the desert with Uncle Vito before returning to Silicon Valley and, as Rhonda described it, "settling in on land again."

The dinner conversation mainly focused on Lisa and me filling them in on our doings the last seven years. When the conversation had veered towards what they had been doing, they would nudge it back into our court.

"I've had an offer to write a book about our adventures," Nick said as I poured each of us a glass of Duncan Gold's finest Cabernet. "They think they could bundle it into a made-for-TV movie deal."

"Are you going to do it?"

"No. We don't need the money and don't want the notoriety."

"But it must be a great story," I said, urging him on. I wanted to hear more of it.

"Uncle Vito said you'd figured out what happened with Samson," he said.

I nodded. I knew Buck Peters had killed Samson because he would not leave Nick's daughter alone. What I didn't know was whose idea it was, Nick's, Buck's, maybe Rhonda's? If not Nick's, did he know about it before Buck shot Samson? What I did know was that I'd never ask Nick those questions.

"Buck beat it overland to Tijuana, and Rhonda, Diego and I headed in that direction in my boat. Buck got there first, rented a small boat, and waited for our call. We picked him up a few miles due west of Tijuana, and headed south."

"When did you rename the yacht?"

"Almost right away, at a boatyard near Ensenada. I knew they'd be looking for the *Opium III*. I chose *Harbor Rat* for the fun of it."

Nick and I had a standing joke, referring to the money people invested in our deals as opium, o-p-m, for "other people's money." He had named his ever-more-expensive yachts Opium in honor of the other people whose money he had leveraged to pay for them. And when we were kids in Seaford, New York, Nick lived south of Merrick Road by the water. That section of town was called Seaford Harbor and we called the kids that lived there harbor rats.

"I loved the photo," I said. Two years after Nick vanished, I got a photo in the mail. It showed Nick, Rhonda, Buck and Diego by a yacht I recognized, but with the new name *Harbor Rat*. "That let me know you were okay."

Nick raised his glass in a toast. I raised mine back. We both needed refills, which I attended to.

"What did you do for seven years?"

"We just tooled around the South Pacific. There are an amazing number of islands between South America and New Zealand, and not too many people."

"You had new identities?"

"Yeah. We had some fun with that, too. Buck became Bubba Smith because he liked the big old football player as an actor. Rhonda became Brenda Johnson, because she had a childhood friend with that name so she thought it would be easy to remember. And I was Vic King," he said, smiling broadly.

"After the Seaford Vikings," I said, nodding appreciatively. Vikings was our high school nickname, and the mighty Viking was our mascot. "What about Diego?"

"Diego said he was too old to remember a new name. We figured that no one was looking for him anyway. I mean, he'd been in the States decades as an undocumented alien, and had been pretty much invisible."

"So what's Buck going to do now?"

"I gave him and Diego the yacht. They plan to change the name again and start a charter service in the islands. They both like the boating life. But I think Rhonda and I have had our fill of it."

"What's next for you?" I said.

"I'm not sure. But I think I'll marry Rhonda."

"You think?"

"Okay, okay, I will marry Rhonda."

"Does she know that?"

"Yeah, she's probably plotting with Lisa about it as we speak."

"How is Uncle Vito doing?"

Nick looked pained. "Not good. As soon as we got here, I talked to him on the phone. He sounded so awful, I caught the next flight to Phoenix. I spent a couple of hours with him, then flew back. He looks awful, lost a lot of weight. He's got some kind of cancer but he won't talk about it."

"I guess we ought to go see him," I said.

"Make it soon. I don't think he has a lot of time left."

"I have to admit, your plan to bring them home was brilliant."

We were reading in bed after saying good-bye to Nick and Rhonda and tidying up. "You have to?" I said.

She gave me her impish grin. "Sometimes, you manage to get it right."

"Well, it wasn't my plan. It was Kyle's."

"Just take the credit, bub," Lisa said. "Face it, this kind of stuff is what you're good at."

"What kind of stuff is that?"

"You know what I mean, buster. Solving thorny problems with clever plans. It is who you are."

This got me to talking about what my shrink had said about needing to integrate my inner Spock with my inner Kirk. "She's right. I have to do that, to be able to trust my own judgement again. First the Woodchipper Incident. Then the Halloween Explosion. Why do I get us into these things?"

"Like I said, it is who you are," Lisa said.

We read for a while.

"You know, there's a reason Kirk is the captain," Lisa said. She went back to her reading.

I put my Kindle down. *Huh!* My mind was racing. It was like suddenly seeing how to solve a puzzle and then rushing to get all the pieces in their places.

Spock was half-Vulcan, half-Human, but he did not trust his human emotions. He suppressed them in favor of Vulcan logic. Kirk was human. Like me, he brought logic and emotion to everything he did. In any situation, he was always faced with the human need to balance the two.

I'd been beating myself up for being impulsive, but Kirk wasn't impulsive. He was a man of action. He was the kind of man you need to "boldly go."

I hadn't acted impulsively in the actions I'd taken that led to the Halloween Explosion. I had actually agonized for some time about what to do. Okay, I had made a bad decision, a fatally bad one. Lisa had always said it was the price I had to be willing to pay to be a leader. To boldly go.

I had learned from my mistakes. It was time to move on.

Chapter 16

When I told Lisa about Uncle Vito's health, she said, "Let's not wait."

So here we were the next Saturday flying to Arizona in Lisa's Cessna. I wanted to use a company Gulfstream, but Lisa wouldn't hear of it.

"This isn't business, so you have to reimburse MySlice, right?"

"We can afford it," I'd said.

"And those pilots probably could use the weekend off," she continued, as if I hadn't said a word.

I knew I was going to lose. Lisa would tolerate my phobia of small planes only so far. She'd usually let me weasel out of flying to the winery with her, accepting my excuse that our work schedules wouldn't match and were subject to change.

But we had an open weekend, the flying distance was well within range for her Skyhawk, and she would not take no for an answer.

As Lisa did her pre-flight whatever, I swallowed some Ativan and made sure for the umpteenth time that the pill container was full and safely tucked in my pocket.

Small prop planes freak me out. I'm fine for a few minutes, able to calm my mind and convince myself that everything was going to be fine. But at the very first air bump, however small, I lose it. Little prop planes always experience bumps and flutters, and my body is exquisitely tuned to detecting the smallest perturbation. In fact, I should enter a study of some sort, I was such a finely tuned instrument.

Once I lose it, I become a basket case. Cold sweat, heart racing, stomach jumping around like an excited puppy, visions of plummeting to earth—and those are the good parts. Worst of all, it doesn't stop until we're on the ground.

I've tried every imaginable distraction and calming technique. None could fool the part of me who is certain we are at most seconds away from plunging to a horrible death.

Today I was giving drugs a try. My doctor had suggested Ativan. If it didn't work, I was in for four hours of pure misery.

Ativan sure did the trick. I felt like I was an observer of the harrowing ride, not a participant. I was sort of outside floating on a cloud while the fools inside the plane were risking their lives. Even when our little plane skipped and fluttered along the thermal waves rising from the desert, I dreamily enjoyed the ride.

Lisa and I were picked up at the Phoenix Deer Valley Airport that afternoon by Kyle's grandfather. Eddie was in his seventies and had a thick Brooklyn accent. As always, he looked cool and dapper. He wore a sharp tan suit and tie with a crisp white shirt.

The air-conditioning in the tan Lincoln Town Car was cranked up to maximum in its battle with the unrelenting desert sun that baked the outdoors at 110 degrees. Sure, it was dry heat, but regardless, it was an oven out there.

Eddie wanted to hear about Kyle, and Lisa and I said all the good things that were guaranteed to warm a grandpa's heart. When Lisa asked how Uncle Vito was doing, all he said was, "The boss is not so good." Then he changed the subject to how great it had been to see Nick again.

Each time I arrive at Uncle Vito's isolated desert compound, I have the same thought: the place looks like a prison. Several acres of barren desert were enclosed by a 12-foot high chain link fence topped with razor wire. Armed guards and patrolling dogs completed the effect.

The sign at the gate read Tan Limousine Service. A square, two story adobe building sat in the center of the property. The first floor had some sort of office in the front. Behind the office, along both sides, ran a series of wide, industrial garage doors. The building was surrounded on all sides by about fifty feet of smooth blacktop. The second floor housed Uncle Vito's private quarters.

Instead of vigorously striding across the shimmering blacktop to greet us as he'd always done before, Lisa and I were escorted upstairs into a sitting room. Uncle Vito was seated in a recliner with an Indian blanket on his lap. The air conditioning was running, but the room felt hot and stuffy, yet Uncle Vito wore a sweatsuit and had on heavy socks and fleece-lined moccasins.

It had been a couple of years since I'd last seen Uncle Vito. I still pictured him as the big man I'd known since I was a child visiting at Nick's house. He'd been built like Babe Ruth, with a barrel chest and spindly legs. He'd had a jowly face with a nose that was mashed and bent to one side, and a ruddy, red complexion. He'd had a thick head of black hair that would have done Ronald Reagan proud. Now it was wispy and gray. He had always looked scary as hell. Now he seemed shriveled and shrunken, like someone had deflated the old Uncle Vito. Nick had told me how he looked, but I still wasn't prepared for the reality I saw.

He didn't rise to greet us. Instead, he lifted his hand in a sort of wave, smiled and said, "Lisa, Michael, how good o' ya to visit an old man." His voice had always been low and gravely. Now it was just above a whisper.

Uncle Vito's first interest was our grandson. Lisa happily obliged, showing him all sorts of photos and videos she had on her phone, while she gushed about the cutest, brightest, most talented baby in the history of our species. Uncle Vito showed keen interest and made appropriate comments of admiration.

When the Brian show wound down, Uncle Vito said, "Ya staying 'til tomorrow, right?"

"Yes, we are," I said.

"Good, good. We're gonna have a real meal tonight. I don't eat so much anymore, but tonight I got Eddie's wife makin' gravy."

Gravy means slow-cooked Italian tomato sauce with meatballs and sausage. Unless otherwise mentioned, spaghetti is presumed, though other pasta is acceptable. We were going to eat very well tonight. I could already taste the onion, garlic and basil in the thick sauce. I wondered if I'd be able to taste the oregano.

"And we got a case of that Cabernet of yours," he said to Lisa. "You make some great wine. I even joined your wine club."

"Thank you. I enjoy making it," Lisa said, "and I really love knowing you appreciate it."

"Yeah, well, that's one thing I still enjoy, my vino. So how about that *schvartze* Nicholas is gonna marry? She's quite a gal."

Like my parents, Uncle Vito grew up in Brooklyn tenements where Jewish and Italians immigrants struggled to make it in their new country. Negroes, as African-Americans were then called, were referred to as *schvartzes*, a Yiddish word borrowed from the German word for black. I had not kept up on politically correct Yiddish, but in Uncle Vito's world, the word was descriptive, not derogatory.

"We like Rhonda a lot," Lisa said. "And Nick loves her."

"Yeah, well, the world's changin', ya know? Even an old fart like me's gotta change with it. And my sister, she's got the family in line."

Nick's mother, Uncle Vito's sister, had laid down the law to her extended family. They were going to accept Rhonda with open arms or face her wrath. Only a fool would choose the latter.

"Mama Marchetti is a force of nature," I said.

"You don't know the half of it. Anyways, speaking of things changin', whodda thought a Jewish kid and a Mexican would be running a big pizza outfit?" Uncle Vito, who had never met Paco Cruz, let himself have a hearty laugh at this crazy new world.

Sensing that our host was tiring, Lisa said, "Do you mind if we freshen up a bit? I think Mike could use his afternoon nap."

We got together again before dinner.

"Your room's okay?"

"It's lovely," Lisa said.

"Listen, I don't know how much time I have left. They wanted to do all sorts of stuff, radiation, chemo, but maybe I'd get a few more months, ya know? For sure, I'd be sick as a dog. So I told 'em no. I'm gonna die here, in my place, with my people. When it's your time, it's your time."

"We're going to miss you," I said.

He waved his hand as if to wave away the sentiment. "Michael, there's some stuff I wanna talk to you about."

Uncle Vito had business to discuss. He was talking to me, but he was honoring Lisa by letting her listen to our business. Gender roles in his world were still pretty rigid.

"You're part of the family, since you were a kid. Anyways, I got some, ah, assets, and I told Nicholas what I want after I go. He's gettin' it all set up. See, I wanna take care of the fellas."

Uncle Vito explained that he wanted to take care of the men who came with him from New York when he retired from the mob and came west. He was going to turn Tan Limousine Service into a partnership, with Nick as general partner. All the men would have shares. They would be guaranteed jobs as long as they were able to work and would also get their shares of the profits even if they could no longer work. The company already owned all the vehicles, equipment and property associated with it.

"Nicholas knows how to do this sorta stuff, ya know? Thing is, what if somethin' happens to him? So I wanna ask you to be a general partner with him. I mean, I just want you two to make the big decisions. You gonna hire someone to run the thing, maybe give 'em a share. And don't worry, Tan Limo is a clean operation, 100% legit."

Uncle Vito's request took me completely by surprise. I looked over at Lisa. She gave a slight nod.

"Thank you," I said. "I'd be honored."

"Ya sure it's gonna be okay for the CEO of MySlice to be, ah, associated with a fella with my past?"

"Thanks for thinking about that. It'll be okay, and if it isn't, I'll deal with it."

"Good, good. Now, look, I'm not gonna have a big funeral. I don't want a circus with the FBI and bloggers and whoever taking pictures of everyone who comes and goes to see who was involved with the old mobster. So I'm asking you not to come to the little ceremony when it happens. That kind of public connection to me, you don't need."

"But..."

He held up his hand. "Do your old uncle a favor, Michael. No buts on that."

"Okay," I said, but I didn't like it.

"The other thing is, Nicholas still owes you. Always will. He knows it, but I know how you fellas are, you're real men, you never talk about it. But I told him, make sure ya never forget ya owe Michael no matter what."

He wasn't referring to me helping Nick return home from being on the run. This debt went back to our senior year in high school. Nick had gotten mixed up with some friends who had gotten advanced copies of their math and science midterm exams. They spent the night before the final memorizing the answers.

They all agreed that they would each get a few answers wrong, to avoid suspicion. But they were high school kids, and their adolescent brains made each think the others would keep that agreement, so they didn't have to. Each went for the best grade possible.

When a dozen boys got nearly perfect scores on the math and science midterms, scores that often far exceeded past performance, the game was over. It was not long before the truth came out and they were all expelled. None graduated with their class. It was a major town scandal, dubbed Exam Scam, and a disgrace for all the boys' families.

But Nick was never included in the investigation. That was because, as a member of the honor society, I helped grade non-honors class exams. I had found out about what the guys were up to and changed enough of Nick's answers so he got the solid B he usually got.

Nick's debt to me was one that no one outside the Marchetti family could possibly fully understand. Nick was going to be the first man in the family to get out of the business, meaning working for the mob that ran the New York docks or working for the union or as a longshoreman, which amounted to pretty much the same thing. Nick was going to go to college and get a white-collar profession.

When Nick saw what happened to the other kids, what it meant to be kicked out of school your senior year, he had grown up fast. Scholarships were cancelled. College acceptances were out the window. Families moved out of town in shame. He suddenly understood what adults meant about the choices you make impacting the rest of your life. I had saved him from that disgrace, and had let him fulfill his family destiny and preserve his family's honor.

It was our secret, but somehow Uncle Vito had found out. Nick got the scholarship to Notre Dame, he got a profession, and he moved west and became wildly successful. I knew that, to Nick and Uncle Vito, Nick owed me a debt of honor. It was a very Italian thing.

"You know Nick saved my life when we were teenagers," I said. Which was true. A guy was about to slit my throat with a knife when Nick whacked him over the head with a two-by-four. As far as I was concerned, we were more than even.

"Yeah, well, that don't change anything. Besides ya just did it again. Ya cleared him and brought him home."

"That was Kyle's plan. I just helped a little. So did you."

Uncle Vito shook his head until his wattle flapped. "The debt still stands. It's not yours to cancel."

We got home Sunday evening after picking up some Chinese food on the way home from the airport. Ativan had again conquered my fear of small plane flying, and I had a good appetite. We were once more eating dinner in the breakfast room. The room did not seem to care which meal it was.

"You don't live in a fortress like that just because you're old and a bit paranoid. Mafia dons don't easily retire," I said.

"Yes," Lisa said.

"He was a major mob boss," I said. "With all that implies."

"I know."

"I don't condone that."

"I know that, too."

"But I've used his muscle and connections from time-to-time."

"When you had to."

"Maybe I had to. Maybe I just chose to."

"It's not a simple world," Lisa said softly.

We shared a bit of silence.

"No matter what," I said, "to me, he's always been my Uncle Vito. From as far back as I can remember."

"What were you two talking about when we left?"

"Well, I hugged him, and it was like holding a small child, not the big strong man I'd always known. I guess he sensed my surprise when I hugged him, and he started chuckling.

"He said, 'Don't sit shiva for me.' I knew what he meant. Don't go into mourning. Then he said, 'Michael, I want to ask a favor.'"

"What did he ask?" Lisa said.

"He said, 'One day, when you take that grandson of yours to see Santa Claus, tell him about Uncle Vito, who played Santa when you were little like him.'"

At Christmas, Uncle Vito would dress up as Santa Claus and arrive at Nick's house in his big Cadillac that seemed a block long, with a trunk full of really cool gifts that he'd hand out to any kid who came by. He made his driver, a hood named Vinnie, wear an elf's hat. A remarkable number of kids just happened to drop by the Marchetti's on Christmas Day.

"You've told me that story a few times," Lisa said with a smile. "He meant a lot to you."

"He did. Still does. He was always this big, scary looking, yet kind and loving man. I learned so much from him about what it means to be a man, to have honor, to keep your word and help your family."

"Like what he's doing for his limo company guys."

"Exactly like that. That's what I mean."

"He's always been there for you."

"Always. When I needed him the most."

"A man full of contradictions," Lisa said.

"Yeah. And all he wants from me is to remember him to Brian as a guy who played Santa Claus."

Chapter 17
Green Zone, Baghdad, Iraq
2006

Colonel Mackenzie Durant sat behind the worn wooden table that served as a desk in his office at U.S. Army Criminal Investigation Command (CID) headquarters in Baghdad. The stack of files on his desk contained the investigative reports of what had become known as the Abu Ghraib Scandal. He closed the final folder and sighed deeply. *What a fucking mess.* He hoped to close the book on it today.

The impetus for the investigation had come from an MP, later known as the Whistleblower of Abu Ghraib, who at the time was serving as a guard at the prison. He had come to be in possession of the damning photos much by accident when he'd borrowed a friend's camera to take some pictures of the infamous Iraqi prison to show the folks back home.

When he'd seen a gallery of photos of naked men in demeaning sexual poses and other acts of torture and abuse, he'd been shocked. What they depicted violated everything he believed in and had been indoctrinated in about the rules of war. He'd seen no such activity in his assigned sector. He had brought his evidence to Adrian Hightower, a CID investigator assigned to Abu Ghraib prison.

Hightower had proceeded with a careful, methodical investigation. He was a by-the-book guy. As his reports went up the chain of command, they stopped at Colonel Durant's desk. Durant had recognized the powder keg they were uncovering. He'd alerted his superior, and soon found himself crafting a carefully worded statement for release to the press. Several drafts had bounced between him and his superior, and, he assumed, right up the chain, probably all the way to the Secretary of Defense.

In January, 2004, Colonel Durant had released the statement in as routine a manner as possible. Opening another folder, he extracted a page and reread it.

An investigation has been initiated into reported incidents of detainee abuse at a Coalition Forces detention facility. The release of specific information concerning the incidents could hinder the investigation, which is in its early stages. The investigation will be conducted in a thorough and professional manner.

As intended, this bland announcement was largely ignored by news media worldwide.

The case had plodded along, and Colonel Durant had done all in his power to see to it that it moved even more slowly than CID's usual plodding pace. He had taken the unusual step of having Hightower report directly to him. Colonel Durant, being a busy man, had then been understandably slow to respond to Hightower's needs for direction. When he had done so, he had often asked for ever more picayune information requiring additional time-consuming investigation.

Colonel Durant had been following his superior's clear but unspoken, unwritten direction: keep a lid on the investigation and make it take as long as possible. And, in clear violation of regulations, no more reports were to go up the chain beyond Colonel Durant. The buck stopped at him. And, in the Army, where the buck stopped, the blame stopped.

The containment effort had come undone a few months later, when *60 Minutes* blew the lid off the scandal with a segment that included graphic pictures of prisoners in all manner of abusive poses. Those images instantly spread around the world and a flood of reporting followed. To this day, Durant had no idea where the leak came from.

Enough reminiscing, he thought. *Time to get on with it.*

Sergeant Adrian Hightower entered Colonel Durant's office and stood at attention.

"At ease, Sergeant. Please sit."

"Yes sir, Colonel! Thank you, sir!"

Sergeant Hightower took in the spartan office. The thick dun-colored stone walls, floor and ceiling were immaculately clean. In addition to the wooden desk, there were three straight-backed, wooden chairs. The Colonel sat in one, and Hightower lowered himself into one of the other two on his side of the desk. In one corner were three mismatched dented metal file cabinets. A power strip snaked across the floor from the room's only electrical outlet. Plugged into it were a desk lamp, laptop computer and shredder.

"You've done a commendable job, Sergeant. What no one wants is to have a repeat of the whistleblower's situation."

As authorized by Colonel Durant, Sergeant Hightower had promised the whistleblower anonymity at the outset of the investigation. He had watched in dismay as Secretary of Defense Donald Rumsfeld later outed the whistleblower during televised testimony before a Senate committee, thanking him for his role in exposing the Abu Ghraib affair.

A hero to many, the Whistleblower of Abu Ghraib had been vilified by others. Things had gotten so bad for him among his fellow soldiers that the Army had sent him home. There, the situation for him and his wife had become ugly, so much so that the Army had taken the highly unusual step of assigning armed protection and helping them relocate.

"Your investigation has resulted in a dozen court-martial convictions, and several more are underway," the Colonel said solemnly. "We've also seen several high level demotions, and you know in the Army that's a career-killer."

The Colonel clasped his hands together and leaned over them, almost prayerfully. "I understand that you have received death threats."

Hightower thought this was disingenuous, as another CID investigator had been looking into them and surely Colonel Durant had seen the reports. Some of the threats had been in anonymous notes, others had come from the mouths of some he had investigated and who had been court-martialed. And he had told the investigator he feared for his life and wanted protection.

"Yes, sir, I have."

"We want you safe, Sergeant. We also frankly do not want you on television giving interviews."

Once outed, the whistleblower had become a media darling, giving high-profile interviews and keeping Abu Ghraib in the public eye."

"Yes, sir!"

"Here's the deal, Sergeant. You are going home. You'll be discharged. If you wish, the Army will help you relocate. You'll agree to keep your role in this investigation and all matters pertaining to it completely confidential. Any questions?"

"Sir, if I may. After the vile rants I've seen online, I would also like help establishing a new identity."

The Colonel squinted at Hightower, then slowly nodded. "We can make that happen."

"Yes, sir! Thank you, sir!" *California, here I come!*

A week before, Hightower had handed Colonel Durant a flash drive. On it was detailed documentation of the orders that Hightower had received that at first slowed the investigation, then shaped its course. It left little to the imagination. Colonel Durant had not only controlled the pace of the investigation, he had intervened to assure who was charged, and, importantly, who was not. He had used every tool of military bureaucracy to micromanage the investigative documents, confining the scope of culpability to the lowest possible links on the chain of command. As little mention was made of the CIA or anyone in Washington as possible. He had put a lid on the damage, at least insofar as it came out of his unit.

He had given Colonel Durant the flash drive without comment, after being dismissed at the end a routine meeting between the two of them. Durant had looked at him quizzically. Hightower had said, "This copy is for your eyes only, sir. It's important." The word "copy" was carefully chosen. Colonel Durant had clearly gotten the message. Adrian Hightower had him by the balls.

Chapter 18

Adrian Harrison Hightower, scion of the Newport Hightowers, had been nothing but a disappointment to his family. His parents traced their lineage on both sides in unbroken lines to the early Newport settlers in the 17th century. These hearty colonists acquired land and became merchants, and as Newport prospered, they became wealthy.

The Hightower fortune grew immensely in the late 1700's and early 1800's, built on the slave trade by shrewd and ruthless Abraham Cushing Hightower. Though trading in slaves was illegal, Newport accounted for nearly half the slave trade in North America, and Abraham Hightower financed a good portion of the ships that carried Hightower rum to Africa and exchanged it for Negro slaves. It was only when the slave trade became unfashionable that old Abraham sold off his rum factories and slave ships, and retired into genteel respectability.

With each succeeding generation, the families became more and more aristocratic. As the inherited wealth accumulated, the men migrated from being tradesman and landlords to bankers and lawyers. Their women ran the top rung of blue-blooded Newport society.

It was assumed that Adrian would follow in his father's footsteps. Yale law school, then a partnership in Hightower Strong, the family white-shoe law firm—Strong was his mother's maiden name, the founding Strong was her grandfather. But it was not to be.

Young Adrian was a polite, well-behaved boy. He did well enough in school—it was not expected that a Hightower would be a top student; that was for the Jewish kids. Regardless, Hightower men always went to Yale, their admissions assured by their legacy status and generous donations. But Adrian dropped out during his freshman year. He came home for Christmas vacation and, when it was time to return to school, matter-of-factly informed his parents that he would not do so.

The furor that erupted was unprecedented in his family, where patrician manners and flat affect ruled behavior. His stately mother, always a bit distant—children were raised by servants, after all—simply stopped speaking to him; he hardly noticed. But his father was another story. He ranted daily at Adrian, making it clear that he was beyond a disappointment, he was somehow ruining the family. Didn't he realize his responsibility as the only son to carry on in the family tradition?

He had a younger sister, but roles and expectations in his family were rigidly based on gender. So she could not fill the void he was creating. She was the only one in the family who asked him why he was dropping out of college. The only one who thought it was about him, not about them. But he had no answer to the why question. He had just woken up one morning in his dorm and realized he was certain he did not want to be there. Where he wanted to be, he had no clue.

"Is it because you're gay?" she'd asked him.

"No, that's not it."

"Mom and Dad still don't know?"

"Of course not. Let's keep it that way."

But he was fed up with his parents. He decided it was time to escape. Impulsively, he joined the Army. That finally shut up his father. After he told them he'd enlisted, he never spoke to his parents again.

Adrian liked the Army. He knew how to show respect to his superiors and found it easy to comply with the regimentation. He took a lot of abuse from his fellows soldiers, who found his upper-class mannerisms amusing. This caused Adrian to experience a new phenomenon: introspection. He got a quick education from his buddies about how the other half—more like the other 99%—live. He came to understand how his life of privilege had insulated him from the real world.

He'd had a lot of practice keeping his sexual orientation hidden. He had no problem living under "Don't ask, don't tell."

His military service led him into the Army Criminal Investigation Command. There, three traits worked in his favor. He was a fanatical record keeper. He wrote down everything, and kept his notes organized. He kept a detailed personal calendar. The second trait was his tenacity. When he set his mind to a task, he pursued it with dogged determination. Third, he was disarmingly likable, which led the subjects of his investigations to let their guards down.

His meticulous documentation of the Abu Ghraib investigation gave him the ammunition he needed to get Colonel Durant to give him a discharge, protection and a new identity. The latter meant he could start over, not as highborn Adrian Hightower of Newport, Rhode Island, but as plain old Sam Jones, small-time tech investor in Silicon Valley, California. The break with his family and heritage was complete.

Sam loved hanging out with tech entrepreneurs. They liked hanging with him, he was a nice guy and a potential investor, so what's not to like? Being a gay man is Silicon Valley was hardly noteworthy.

Most of his investments became worthless, quietly petering out when they hit the magic three-year mark that seems to sort out the few tech startup winners from the many losers. But the amounts he invested were small, at most a few hundred thousand dollars at a time, and he did have a few winners. Enough to enable him to live the lifestyle he wanted and keep his nest egg intact. As he got better at his profession, the next egg began to grow.

And it was a substantial nest egg.

Chapter 19
Baghdad, Iraq
2003-2006

Operation Iraqi Freedom, the invasion of Iraq by the U.S. and its coalition, began with bombing missions on March 19, 2003. That same day, a handwritten note was received by the Iraqi Central Bank. Translated, it read as follows:

> Extremely confidential. In the name of God the most merciful the most compassionate. Mr. Governor of the Iraqi central bank. We are giving, with this written note, permission to Mr. Qusay Saddam Hussein and Mr. Hekmat Mizban Ibrahiem to receive the following amounts of money:
> 1-Nine hundred and twenty million American dollars.
> 2-Ninety million Euros.
> To protect and save them from American aggression. Take the necessary action.
> (signed) Saddam Hussein, President of the Republic

According to captured Finance Minister Hekmat Mizban Ibrahim al-Azzawi, later that day the money was placed in stainless steel briefcases, a million dollars or euros per case. It was then carted away on three flatbed trucks.

U.S. military forces eventually recovered nearly all of this cash, but, to this day, 132 million dollars is unaccounted for. It is thought to have ended up in the hands of Iraqi insurgents, and is believed to have funded their early efforts.

Alvin Baxter was deployed in an advance M.P. unit that arrived in Baghdad in early April, 2003. All hell was breaking loose in the Iraqi capital. The Iraqi military had crumbled, there was no government, and chaos and disorder reigned. U.S. military police were playing whack-a-mole, and there were way more moles than M.P.s

Baxter's six man M.P. unit was tasked with guarding a truck that had been found on the grounds of Saddam Hussein's palace, loaded with 319 cases of neatly packed hundred dollar bills. The money was in packets of 100 bills, $10,000 to a packet, 100 packets—a million dollars—to a case. They were guarding 319 million dollars in cash.

When Baxter's unit was relieved a week later, the truck contained 309 cases. Somehow, the paperwork that Baxter handed off to their relief showed that to be the original figure.

During that week, he had surreptitiously liberated 10 million dollars. Ten steel cases had disappeared, their contents transferred to four common military duffel bags whose contents weighed over 50 pounds each. Baxter did not mind the weight.

Over the next few weeks, Baxter played an unnerving game of hide-the-duffel-bags. Then he had the good fortune to be assigned as a guard at Abu Ghraib prison. Originally built by the British in the 1950s, it had become Saddam Hussein's house of horrors until, facing imminent U.S. invasion, he granted amnesty to all its inmates and released them. As U.S. Army forces moved into Iraq, the empty prison started filling up with prisoners of interest to the U.S. Army and CIA.

The prison, which at its peak had housed 15,000 inmates, was a maze of cellblocks, storage rooms, guard dorms, kitchens and other support facilities. It also had six partially completed new cellblocks that Saddam had begun building the year before he reversed course and emptied the prison. It was in the chaos of this new construction that Baxter hid his loot.

How do you smuggle four duffle bags full of hundred dollar bills out of wartime Iraq?

You'd think it would be easy. The Army has hundreds of thousands of duffel bags and they all look alike. And with so much gear going back and forth between the U.S. and Iraq, who would take notice of four more? Baxter knew better. The Army was fanatical about preventing any wartime booty, from antiquities, artwork, weapons and souvenirs to stolen currency, from getting into the U.S. from Iraq. The baggage of soldiers returning to the States was screened by hand. Shipments home were meticulously inspected. Already, there had been attempts to smuggle contraband in body bags containing corpses, in supposedly empty cargo containers, and by other creative means. As these were foiled, they were publicized in the ranks to be sure the message came through loud and clear: Don't even think about trying it.

Baxter's answer to how to smuggle the loot home was to wait. So long as he kept the money hidden, he could afford to wait for an opportunity to arise. If that didn't happen if he had to do something risky, he figured he could always do that later.

A year later, Alvin Baxter was one of the guards swept up in the investigation of Abu Ghraib prisoner abuse. When investigator Adrian Hightower came across his name, it seemed strangely familiar. When he got out of bed the next morning, the memory was clear.

In 2003, Hightower had been assigned to investigate the disappearance of about 130 million dollars in cash from the funds Saddam Hussein had withdrawn from the Iraqi Central Bank when the war started. He was actually impressed that nearly a billion dollars had been recovered, given the chaos that reigned in the first days of the Battle of Baghdad. But he could never pin down where the still missing cash had gone. With the subtle encouragement of his superiors, he had concluded that it most likely had fallen into the hands of the nascent Iraqi insurgency movement.

When Hightower checked his files, he confirmed what he had remembered overnight. Specialist Alvin Baxter had been one of the men assigned to guard a truck containing over a third of a billion dollars in cash.

On a hunch, he carefully looked through that file again. With the help of a magnifying glass and a light box, he saw where the one had been changed to a zero on the paperwork. So 319 steel cases had become 309. Ten missing cases, 10 million dollars in cash.

After a time, the deal with Baxter was struck. For one million dollars, Adrian would assure that the cash got safely into the United States. He would also see to it that Baxter was exonerated for his role in the Abu Ghraib atrocities.

There is a large warehouse at the U.S. Army Criminal Investigation Command headquarter in Quantico, Virginia. In it are kept the records of closed CID investigations. These records are stored in standard issue cartons, stacked on twelve foot high metal shelving units, acres upon acres of them.

Access to these records requires verification of authorization by case number. Adrian would create a dummy case number and ship the money to Quantico in sealed records cartons. He would get himself sent home, then he would withdraw those boxes from storage. He was certain that Colonel Durant would sign the necessary authorization form without even reading it.

But Hightower did not explain these details to Baxter. All he told him was that, because of his role in CID, he had

114

a foolproof way to get the cash home and, later, into his hands. Hightower would take his cut and store the remaining nine million in a safe deposit box for Baxter. It would be there when he returned home.

But Baxter was court martialed, convicted and sentenced to eight months in prison and a dishonorable discharge. What could he do, claim that Adrian had double-crossed him and admit to yet another major offense?

By the time Baxter was out of the stockade and discharged, Adrian Hightower and the 10 million dollars had vanished.

When Sam Jones first arrived in Silicon Valley, he had no idea what to do with his cash hoard. He knew he couldn't just spend cash for everything. He knew he couldn't deposit it in banks without attracting unwanted attention. But he was clueless about how to launder the money.

Then he saw a storefront that said CASH on the front window in huge letters. *Okay,* he thought, *there's a clue.* Soon, he had learned about the world of payday loans, check cashing, and other services provided to the poor and undocumented who didn't have bank accounts. Over the next few months, Jones bought five of these establishments in barrios from Stockton to Salinas. Their price—in cash— was cheap.

In each shop, he hired a manager and installed tight systems along with cameras that took continuous videos of the action inside. Then he cooked the books. With so many small cash transactions, he was easily able to augment the take of each shop with his stolen cash. In this fashion, he laundered a total of about a million dollars a year of the stolen money.

Nearly a decade later, he sold those shops. They had served their purpose; the cash from Iraq had all been cleansed.

Oddly, the new owner could not reproduce the profits Sam had been able to generate.

Chapter 20

Sam Jones was getting a bad case of cabin fever.

He'd recovered enough from surgery that he no longer needed to be in a hospital. It was time to work out where he would go to recuperate. The issue was security. It had taken several days for him to come out of his post-operative stupor, but when he did he realized his peril.

He thought about how he'd landed in this fix. The conversation had seemed innocent enough. Brandetti had seemed to finally grasp that the judge who had been hearing their lawsuit was not going to let him wriggle out of the settlement agreement.

"Oh, what the hell," Brandetti had said, suddenly jaunty. "Let's take a break and then finish this."

The lawyers had pulled out their phones and waved them away. As they left the barn and started along a path between two rows of vines, Sam's cell phone rang. He looked at the caller ID. "I better take this."

Sam stepped away but Brandetti could still hear some of his end of the conversation. He heard Jones say, "No, it's over. It's time to move on."

When the call ended, Brandetti, unashamed of his eavesdropping, said, "Sounded like you were telling some guy you weren't going to back his startup."

"I only wish," Sam said. "I was telling my ex that he and I were really finished."

Brandetti did a double-take when he heard the word "he." Jones had spent enough time with him to know that Brandetti hated Blacks, Jews, Arabs and Muslims. And he wasn't too keen about Asians and Mexicans. Jones should have known that gay men were at the top of Brandetti's hate list. It had just never come up before.

It was bad enough that Jones had him at the end of his rope financially. That the cause of his downfall was also gay pushed Giuseppe Brandetti over the edge. "I've had enough, you queer motherfucker!" he roared.

Leaving a stunned Sam Jones, rooted to the ground, Brandetti had sprinted away, returning in seconds with a gun, and the chase was on.

That was the statement he gave to the cops. He had to repeat it three times, which Sam knew was intended to ferret out inconsistencies. But Sam was good at details, and he kept his story straight.

With the publicity the story was getting and the photos of himself that went with it, Jones had figured it was quite possible that he might be recognized by Alvin Baxter, the man he had swindled a decade earlier.

So Jones had made a phone call. General Durant was his life insurance policy.

The last thing the General wanted was to have Abu Ghraib back in the news as part of a sensational cover-up story, with him as the lead villain. Jones still had copies of that flash drive, and he'd made it clear to Durant that, in the event of his unnatural death, he had arranged that copies would go to several major news outlets. He also said that each was being kept in a different place and had a different delivery mechanism.

Durant knew nothing about Baxter and the 10 million dollars. To him, Baxter was just another grunt swept up in the Abu Ghraib prosecutions. Hightower came from a rich family and Durant assumed that's where he got his money when he became Sam Jones.

Jones hadn't asked him for a thing since he'd been relocated and gotten his new identity. Now it was enough for Durant that Jones was in fear for his life and wanted some protection. The guy was probably just paranoid, but he could easily handle the request.

In the post-9/11 world, a General in uniform making noises about national security got ready cooperation from the hospital administrator. Within hours, Jones had a single room, isolated at the end of a hallway. An Army guard was posted outside his door twenty-four hours a day. Mr. Jones was to have no visitors. No information about his condition was to be given to anyone except that he was stable. And he could stay as long as he wanted, the hospital would eat the costs.

The presence of an armed military guard would itself attract unwanted attention. So the local sheriff was enlisted to help. The guards were given badges and uniforms, and sworn in as special deputies. The cover story was that the guards were a precaution, given that the reason for Brandetti's attack on Jones was still uncertain and others might possibly be involved.

Jones figured that the cover story would soon wear thin. He needed a new plan.

Chapter 21

"I need to ask you for a favor, Jeff."

Lisa and Sheriff Ryder sat on the front porch of Big Vic, looking over the vineyards and sipping Duncan Gold Chardonnay. Ryder was a big man, who swore that his girth was not a beer belly, but rather caused by a hazard of his job. He was constantly being offered wine to taste, and it would be impolite, if not politically inept, to refuse too frequently. Since he viewed making regular visits to local winemakers as an important part of his of job, what was a poor public servant to do?

"Sure, Lisa. How can I help you?"

"I want to get a message to Sam Jones. The hospital won't let me talk to him or even give him a note from me. I thought of writing him a letter and mailing it there, but I'm not sure he'd get it. I understand you have a guard posted outside his room."

Ryder scratched his head. "I do," he said.

"So if I write a note, would you see that he gets it?"

Sheriff Ryder suddenly noticed that their wineglasses needed refilling. He performed the task slowly as he thought about Lisa's seemingly simple request.

The guards really weren't his men, they were the Army's. Would one of them do him the favor of passing a note to Sam Jones? Probably, he concluded. He'd just need to approach the guy right.

"Glad to do that," he said.

Lisa smiled, thanked him, and went inside to write the note.

"So you're the one who saved my life."

Lisa sat at Sam Jones's bedside. She took in the man. His full beard was trim and neatly groomed. He wore sweatpants and a sweatshirt—a good choice, she thought, as the hospital was, as usual, cold. He wasn't hooked up to any monitoring devices or dispensing machines. The only sign that he wasn't perfectly well was the fact that he was in a hospital bed.

"I just did what anyone would do," she said.

"I'm not so sure of that," he said with a warm smile. "In any case, I've been waiting to say thank you."

"I tried to get in to see you sooner, but they said no visitors or phone calls."

He waved dismissively. "They're just being overcautious. Overprotective."

"How are you?"

"Surprisingly well for a guy who was shot three times. One bullet hit me here, bounced off a rib, and passed though." He pointed with his right hand to the spot on his left side. "It cracked a rib, but that's healed.

"Another bullet hit me here." He pointed to his right thigh. "It was what they call a through-and-through. It missed a major artery and just tore up a bit of muscle and fat. Lots of blood, and I'll limp for a few weeks, but if I do my physical therapy, it should be as good as new."

"The third bullet did the real damage." He grabbed his right shoulder with his left hand. "It really messed up my shoulder. They had to do a lot of reconstruction, but if I stick to my PT, I should get it back to eighty percent, maybe more."

"I'm so sorry," Lisa said.

"What for? If not for you, I'd be dead. Which reminds me, where are my manners? How is your head?"

Lisa reflexively touched her hair over the spot. "Oh, it was really nothing, just a scratch. Now that my hair is growing in, I don't even think about it."

"I'm glad for that," he said.

Lisa was dying to ask Jones why Brandetti had shot him. But she decided it was not her place to do so. Instead, she said, "When do you go home?"

"As soon as I get off my butt and make arrangements. I live alone, and I still have some dizziness, probably from the bump to the head when you guys fell down on top of me. So they don't want me left alone yet. I need to arrange for some in-home nursing care and set up physical therapy."

"Why don't you stay at the winery? We have a great residence and a housekeeper who can stay with you. It'll be perfect."

"I could never impose on you like that."

"Don't be silly," Lisa said, warming to the idea. "We have a guest room in our house that still has a hospital bed, from when my husband was recovering from an injury. And we have a pretty well-equipped physical therapy room in one of the outbuildings that Mike used. You could probably use his physical therapist, Janelle. She set the gym up and does house calls."

Well, well, Sam Jones thought. *It looks like my new plan just fell into my lap.*

Chapter 22

Lisa was back home, and I'd made my famous chicken Caesar salad and had picked up a French baguette for dinner. Now we were sitting on our back deck, enjoying the last of the bottle of Duncan Gold Viognier that had accompanied the meal. The evening was lovely, low seventies, a slight breeze, and some birds were chirping goodbye to the sun.

I was day-dreaming a bit, when I realized what Lisa was saying to me. "So Sam Jones is staying at Big Vic?" I said, not hiding my surprise.

"Well, it makes sense," Lisa said. "He needs physical therapy and we have the gym right there."

"I thought that stuff was all being donated."

"It will be in a few weeks. The clinic needs to finish remodeling first to make room."

After the Halloween Explosion, when it became clear that I would need daily physical therapy, we had converted an outbuilding at Duncan Gold Vineyards into a small gym. The building was once a bunkhouse for workers, but for years it had been used to store all sorts of miscellaneous junk. Broken equipment, furniture, tools and odd parts of who-knows-what, just got tossed in.

While I was still in the hospital, Lisa had a hauler clear out everything and got a contractor to refurbish the place. Then she'd worked with Janelle, the physical therapist I'd be using, to outfit it with equipment. When I'd arrived at Big Vic to recuperate, the gym was ready for me.

Then Lisa had a great idea. She contacted a local non-profit agency that provided free medical care for vineyard and winery workers who did not have health insurance or had severe limits on physical therapy visits. These were mainly seasonal workers, often migrant Mexicans, though there were plenty of part-time, uninsured or under insured locals as well. The folks the agency served performed hard physical labor and injuries were all too frequent.

Lisa hooked up the agency with the physical therapy clinic Janelle worked for. The deal she brokered was that we would donate all the equipment in our gym to the clinic after I was finished with it. The clinic would contract with the agency to provide physical therapy for its clients at rock-bottom rates. We sweetened the deal with a five-year pledge to the non-profit for a considerable annual sum earmarked for the physical therapy program.

The day of the vineyard shooting, Lisa was on her way to Yountville to finalize the deal over lunch. But she'd been distracted by the sound of gunshots, and that meeting had been delayed.

"There are physical therapy clinics everywhere." I still wasn't getting this.

"Well, he also has dizzy spells from a bump on the head. So he needs someone around all the time. And Rosa's right there." Lisa used the small voice she uses when she knows what she's telling me sounds lame.

"Rosa's a wonder, but still…"

"I don't know, Mike. He's such a nice guy, and it just seemed like the right thing to do. I had to talk him into it."

"Okay, but this still seems odd to me." I said. "You don't usually take in stray animals, even if they are wounded."

Lisa pulled a face at my analogy. I sensed I was heading for trouble. "So how long does the Big Vic Clinic have this patient?"

"We didn't talk about that," she said sharply.

I was getting snarky, which could not lead to good things. It was time to leave this alone. "What do you hear from Julie?" Changing the subject to Lisa's sister was always a good move.

Chapter 23

Nick, Marty and I were eating lunch that Friday at the Los Gatos MySlice.

"How was the trip?" I said to Nick. He and Rhonda had returned from New York a few days ago after a stop in Arizona to see Uncle Vito.

While Nick was visiting his family, the FBI had announced the arrest of Tracy Luce and the recovery of most of the money she had embezzled from the Zack Zander Foundation. Special Agent in Charge Alex Greene had shared the podium with Zack's mother, who had thanked the FBI and praised them for their diligence.

Marty knew nothing about Nick's connection to that. I knew Nick had been vague about the circumstances leading to his return, and Marty was the kind of friend who understood not to go there.

"I forgot how big my family is." Nick filled me in on various members of his extended clan I knew as a kid growing up. Marty did not know these folks, but he seemed content to focus on his pizza.

"How did it go for Rhonda?" I knew Nick's Italian family. They were warm and loving. They also did not keep their opinions to themselves, and I was anxious about how they'd accept a black woman into the family.

"I think the reality that we were together was different from the idea of it. First thing we did when we got to New York, we went to the diamond district and bought a ring. I wanted to make our relationship clear.

"Momma warmed to her right away. You know, if she could take to an annoying Jewish brat like you, what's the big deal about a black woman?"

Nick's mother had been my second mom. As a kid growing up, I spent almost as much time at his house as my own.

"I had to promise Momma we'd have a big New York wedding. Then she made it clear to everyone that Rhonda was going to be her new daughter-in-law and she was delighted. They got the message."

I laughed. Momma was a sweet, little old Italian lady who seemed mainly interested in making sure everyone was constantly eating, but you crossed her at your peril. So she'd gotten the upcoming wedding she wanted from Nick, and acceptance for Rhonda from everyone else.

"I think I'd like your momma," Marty said.

"You'll meet her at the wedding," Nick said.

We worked on our pizza for a while. The silence was comfortable. But I had some business that I needed to bring up.

"So what do you guys know about Sam Jones?"

I had asked Marty and Nick to check around and see what they could find out about the guy.

"It's no surprise I'd never heard of him," Nick said. "I took off on my little cruise not long after he was getting started in the Valley. Anyway, I've been working the phones, mostly other VCs, reconnecting after seven years."

Nick was the best networker I've ever known. He'd always used the phone to stay in touch with a boatload of people in the tech world by actually talking to them. I didn't think he'd turn to the social media that had emerged while he was away.

"Bottom line is that he's pretty well liked. He's an angel investor. Typical deal is a couple of hundred thousand. Like most angels, he's had a few winners, but mostly losers."

"That's the life of an angel," Marty said. "A lot of small bets, a few big payoffs."

Marty likes to stay connected to entrepreneurial tech folks, especially ones who are involved in startups. He likes their energy, and they like bouncing ideas off him.

"I've run into the guy a few times, but he didn't make much of an impression. He seems to attend every tech get-together in the Valley," Marty said. "Anyplace he can schmooze with guys trying to do startups. Anyway, I asked around. A lot of people know him. You know how popular angels are with guys who want to do a startup. Anyway, no one had anything bad to say. His reputation is that he's a decent guy to deal with and stays out of your hair once he invests."

"I wonder where his money came from." Nick said.

"I wonder why he put two million into a bogus winery deal without doing his due diligence," I said. "He nearly got killed for his trouble."

"His ego got him," Marty said. "He's had success investing in tech startups, so he figures he can invest in any kind of startup."

"A pattern we've seen all too often," I said.

"He probably just wanted to be a wine baron," Nick said. "It's amazing how the glamor and romance of the wine business trips up otherwise smart guys."

"Present company excluded," I said.

"Of course," he said.

Chapter 24

"How are you feeling, Sam?"

"Much better, thanks," Sam Jones said. "Rosa feeds me like crazy and watches me like a hawk. If I didn't get to walk around this beautiful place so much, I'd be getting fat. And Janelle is a cruel taskmaster but she's doing wonders for me. She won't hear about eighty percent recovery. We're going for a hundred percent."

Lisa looked out over the vineyards from Big Vic's front porch. The sun was setting and the vines closest to Big Vic were still heavy with grapes and ready for picking. The vineyard was bathed in soft orange light.

It is beautiful. "How's the dizziness?"

"Gone. You have a real good health spa here. I can't thank you enough, you've been so generous."

"Thanks for helping out in the tasting room."

"I sort of needed something to do, to take my mind off of the shooting."

Lisa had already heard from José, the tasting room manager, that Jones got along well with the tasting room staff and customers, and was actually a real help.

"Sorry about the security problem," she said.

"Not to worry. It wasn't your fault. When the press got wind that I was here, they just got curious. I called the outfit you recommended and they sent someone out right away."

Sam had called Lisa when the press started hassling him. Lisa gave him the name and number of the security firm they had used just a while ago.

"How come you have someone here 24/7?"

Sam shrugged. "I just feel better knowing there's always a guard around. Maybe I'm just skittish after the shooting and all."

Lisa figured if he wanted a bodyguard all the time and was paying for it, she couldn't really object. But it made her feel vaguely uneasy. Even when it was bustling with activity, the winery was a kind of peaceful sanctuary for her. Security guards somehow spoiled that. She disliked using them there and was always happy when they were no longer needed.

"I've been meaning to ask, why did Brandetti shoot you?"

"While we were taking a walk, it came out that I'm gay, which he didn't know. It had just never come up. Turns out the guy hated gays, and I guess it was too much for him that he'd lost that lawsuit to a gay man. He just went nuts."

Lisa remembered the look on Brandetti's face when she got her car between him and Sam that day. His face had been contorted in a hideous expression of fury. *I guess it was hatred and craziness,* she thought.

Lisa was at a loss as to what to say but Sam rescued the conversation.

"You know, your hair looks great. With that short cut, you can't tell part of it had been shaved."

Lisa found herself smiling at the compliment. Sam was sure easy to talk to.

The old guy named Wayne started showing up at the Duncan Gold tasting room about the time Sam Jones moved into Big Vic. Wayne would drop in two or three times a week at different times of the day, taste the wine and schmooze with the servers. They were soon comfortable with the amusing, lonely old veteran, and he quickly graduated to the status of a regular.

When Jones started helping out in the tasting room, Wayne seemed especially drawn to him. Wayne loved to tell war stories, and ragged on Sam unmercifully for his purported lack of military service. Yet, try though he might, he could not get any background on Sam before he came to California.

He did learn a lot about Jones's life since coming to the West. In bits and pieces, never probing too hard, Wayne had been able to flesh out a rather extensive profile of the man.

While Wayne chatted and tasted wine, Baxter loitered in the parking lot. He'd rented a black SUV and a chauffeur's uniform. He kept the brim of the uniform cap pulled low over his eyes, and avoided the tasting room staff. The cover story was that Wayne, though living in independent living at the Veteran's Home, was reasonably well off and used a hired car to get around. Limos and their drivers were commonplace at tasting rooms. No one paid much attention to him.

Baxter especially noted how much time Sam spent with Lisa Gold. Wayne had filled him in on how she flew back and forth between Silicon Valley and Napa Valley. When she was at the winery, she and Jones had lunch on the front porch of the owner's residence nearly every day. And they were sleeping in the same house. They seemed very cozy.

He also took note of the bodyguard who shadowed Jones everywhere. That plus the guards at the hospital told Baxter that Jones was well-protected. He couldn't just snatch the guy and beat on him until he gave up the nine million dollars—plus interest—he owed him. Baxter spent a lot of time in his cheap motel room trying to think of some other way.

Chapter 25

"This is outrageous!"

I slammed the papers Lisa had handed me down on the antique coffee table in Annie Oakley's office. I was so angry I was sputtering.

"It isn't true, Mike," Lisa said. There was a plaintive quality to her voice.

I closed my eyes and worked on slowing my breathing. As I calmed, I realized Lisa and I were not exactly talking about the same thing.

"Honey, what I mean is that the suit is outrageous. I don't believe the crap about you and Jones."

Lisa had called me that morning. All she said was that she'd been served with a notice that she was being sued by Giuseppe Brandetti's estate for wrongful death. A few calls later, we had scheduled to meet Annie in her office in Cupertino early that afternoon. Lisa flew home and drove straight there from the airport, and I cancelled my afternoon appointments and met her there.

Anita Mae Oakley was, as she told it, born dirt poor in a dusty town in east Texas that consisted of a filling station and a six-stool diner, at a crossroads of two-lane highways to nowhere. She says it was so small it didn't have a name.

She was nicknamed Annie Oakley the first day she went to school, which was an hour away by school bus. The new nickname led to numerous fights, which Annie, the tomboy, handled with relish.

As so often happens, the tomboy grew into a very attractive woman. Barely over five feet tall, maybe one hundred pounds, blue eyes and long, thick blond hair. Smart and hyperactive, Annie went to the University of Texas, graduated summa cum laude in three years, and earned a scholarship to Stanford Law School.

After graduation, Annie went to work at a premier Silicon Valley law firm as an associate in its venture law group. Five years later, she turned down the chance to become a partner and opened her own boutique law firm catering to tech start-ups. Over time, her practice had morphed into serving the personal legal needs of successful entrepreneurs from some of those startups. People like Lisa and me.

Over the years, Annie had become a close friend to both of us. We relied on her advice and trusted her completely. Her office is plush, warm, and full of antiques and art. Lisa and I sat together on a low couch, Annie in an arm chair. It was more like being in a tasteful living room than an office. But however soft her decorating taste may be, in a legal fight I want Annie on my side.

I took Lisa's hand as she moved closer to me on the couch. We both turned to face Annie. She addressed Lisa.

"Okay, let me cut through the legal mumbo-jumbo and tell you what this is really all about. The suit is filed by Brandetti's parents, Emma and Tyler Brandet of Silver

City, Nevada. It claims that you and Jones have had a long-standing affair. It claims Brandetti was mentally ill at the time of the shooting incident, caused by the undue stress Jones imposed upon him over their partnership dispute, and that your intervention to save your lover actually caused Brandetti's death. They're seeking 20 million dollars."

"There was no affair," Lisa said with an edge of her own anger. "I never met the man before the shooting."

"And what was Lisa supposed to do, let Brandetti kill Jones?" I said.

"The fact that a claim is stupid, false or insulting doesn't mean it can't be used in a lawsuit. You've been there, Mike."

True. In business, we were sued all the time for the goofiest of reasons. And sometimes I was named personally. I thought about how I knew anyone could sue you at any time for anything, but now that Lisa was the target, I had forgotten that truth and became indignant.

"You two let me worry about this," Annie said. "That's my job. Meanwhile, don't discuss the suit with anyone, even your closest friends and family members. Especially not with Sam Jones. I'll work with his lawyer, but don't assume your interests and his are aligned.

"If you feel you must say something in a situation, just say that the claims are false and your lawyer is handling this annoyance. Which I am. Do not go into any details."

"Will there be a trial?"

"It's too soon to know," Annie said. "Do you want to settle to avoid a trial?"

"No," I said.

"Why not?" Lisa said.

"I don't want to give any credibility to this nonsense," I said.

"But you settle a lot of business lawsuits."

"That's different. That's just good business. This is personal."

"I don't know," Lisa said, looking distressed. "I just want to make these nasty lies go away."

"How about this," Annie said. "Let's see what develops in the next few days."

When we got home, Lisa and I sat in the shade on the front porch loveseat. We had gotten well into a bottle of Duncan Gold Chardonnay without saying much of anything.

"I love you," I said.

"And I love you."

"I'm so sorry this happened."

"Do you think anyone will believe it?"

I knew she meant the affair accusation, not the wrongful death part. That wasn't on her mind.

"I don't believe it," I said. "Never did."

She gave me a weak smile. "Well, that's all that really matters."

"No one who matters will believe it."

"I hope not," she said. "I've been spending too much time at the winery. And when I'm home, I'm off to see the baby."

"And I've been too busy jetting around, showing everyone that MySlice's CEO is back in action."

"We can fix this," Lisa said.

I went inside for another bottle of wine. I added a tray of crackers and cheese. By the time we finished the second bottle, I was getting a much stronger smile.

That same day, Sam Jones was in the tasting room when he was served with the lawsuit, moments after Lisa had been served at Little Vic. Rosa had helpfully told the process server where to find him. Sam and Lisa hadn't even seen each other before she'd left for the airport. He packed, said a warm good-bye to Rosa, and drove home to Los Gatos with his bodyguard at the wheel of his BMW.

Chapter 26

The news of the Gold-Jones lawsuit did not sit well with General Durant. He feared that a trial could easily delve into Sam Jones's past. He did not want anyone going there. He wanted Adrian Hightower to stay buried, for fear he might reveal Durant's murky involvement in the Abu Ghraib investigation.

Durant had first tried to sabotage the Abu Ghraib investigation. When those damning photos became public, he saw to it that his Army superiors, the CIA, and Washington bigwigs were kept out of it as much as possible. For all the shit that actually hit the fan—and there was a ton of it—there was much more that Durant had managed to bury.

As a two-star general in the Army intelligence service, he was now one rung below the top job in the entire Army intelligence apparatus. That was the job he coveted, running what was known as G-2. He also coveted the third star that went with it. That position would put him in charge of all U.S. Army intelligence assets worldwide, including around 30,000 personnel and billions of budget dollars. He wanted that power and prestige before he retired.

So what to do about this damn lawsuit? No matter which way he looked at it, it came down to one of two options: get the Brandets to withdraw the suit, or eliminate them.

The first was actually the more risky choice. He could pay them off, but no matter how much he hid the source of the payoff, they'd still be out there, like ticking time bombs. Installment payments might keep them quiet, but money had a nasty habit of becoming traceable at the most inopportune time.

On the other hand, no Brandets, no one with standing to pursue the suit. The more he thought about it, the cleaner and more appealing that choice looked. Over his career, he'd learned that the simpler the solution to a problem, the less that could go wrong.

He'd also learned that you never have too much intelligence.

The fit-looking young woman shook her head as she parked her SUV in front of the post office in Silver City, Nevada. How this tiny dump merited a post office was beyond her. No wonder they always had budget problems. The town consisted of a few ramshackle buildings, but was mainly a place for tourists to stop and take a leak on their way from Reno to Virginia City, where the glory days of 19th century silver mining were celebrated in tongue-in-cheek Old West style.

All the Ghost had was a post office box number. She got directions to the Brandets by posing as a nurse, saying she had to give them both the last dose of medication to clear up a "private matter." She blushed prettily when she said it. The leathery old gal at the tiny, dilapidated post office looked left, then right—there was no one else there—and whispered the directions. She said they were squatting on some federal land in the hills east of Silver City.

She was glad she had an SUV with high clearance and four-wheel drive. The region was as sparsely populated as the Mojave Desert. Once she got a few of hundred yards out of town, the asphalt road she had been directed to became gravel. A half a mile later, it was dirt, a mere scratch on the barren sunbaked earth.

She drove for about another half hour, carefully checking for the landmarks she'd gotten from the post office lady. She also used the Army's special GPS system linked with Google Earth to stay on course. She hadn't passed a structure or another vehicle in miles when she spotted the sun glinting off a silver trailer several hundred feet off the dirt road. There was no discernable driveway, so she just turned off the road and headed for it.

Except for the tumbleweed, the terrain could have been Martian. She'd been in wastelands before, halfway around the world, but this was right up there on the desolate scale. Who would choose to live here? She was about to find out.

As she approached the trailer, she noticed a badly rusted old brown Ford pickup parked nearby. There was a sort of awning on both sides of the trailer, one providing a spec of morning shade, the other taking over in the afternoon. It being mid-afternoon, two mismatched folding beach chairs were under the east awning, each occupied.

She stopped about 10 feet from the trailer. There was a stale odor of marijuana. A skinny gray mutt approached her listlessly. It yapped a few feeble barks, lost interest, and went back to the shade.

The two chair dwellers looked remarkably alike. Each was rail thin, with long scraggily gray hair in a ponytail and wrinkled, leathery skin. They both wore dirty white tee shirts, faded jeans and scuffed brown work boots. The man had a few days growth of gray beard; the woman did not.

They eyed her with a mixture of suspicion and hostility. Neither spoke or made a move to get up.

"I'm looking for Mr. and Mrs. Brandet," she said.

The woman laughed. It was a gravelly, smoker's laugh. "You see anyone else around here?"

She made a show of shading her eyes with her hand and slowly looking around. "Let me guess. You're Emma, and you, sir, are Tyler."

"Okay, you're a genius," said Emma. "Whadaya want?"

"I'm here to talk to you about the lawsuit you filed concerning your son's death."

It was Tyler's turn to speak. "The last feller bought us a nice dinner afore he got us to sign them papers. He also paid us for our time."

"That sounds like a fine idea," she said.

"Paid us a thousand bucks," Tyler said.

"Well," she said, "I'm good for dinner and five hundred."

"There's a nice place near where 341 meets 50," Emma said. "Just give us a minute to freshen up."

While they were inside, she walked completely around the trailer. There wasn't much to take note of, but you could never be too thorough gathering intel. Then she started the SUV and cranked up the air conditioning.

Freshening up appeared to consist of changing into a clean, colored tee shirt. The Brandets both sat in the back seat, like they were in a limo.

They rode in silence for 10 minutes before Tyler said, "So what's your name?"

"Cleo." She had decided that today she would be Egyptian.

"Got a last name?"

"Tut."

"Cleo Tut," he said. "Funny name."

"My parents were hippies," she said. That line seemed to work in a lot of situations.

The Brandets were not going to talk to her until they ordered their meals. They were taking no chances.

The nice place they directed her to was called Al's and Sal's. It was on route 50, the highway to Reno, between a gas station, designed mainly for eighteen-wheelers, and the Silver Souvies souvenir stand. She wouldn't have stopped there for a meal on her own even if she were starving.

They sat at a well-worn booth with a formica-topped table, replete with cigarette burns. The Brandets each ordered a shrimp cocktail, buffalo wings, a steak with corn-on-the-cob and a baked potato, fried onion rings and a bottle of Bud. She played it safe and got a burger, well done to kill the bacteria, fries and a Coca-Cola.

By the time they considered the dessert menu, she had pieced together the story. A man named Al had visited them a week ago. He said they had grounds to sue some people who had caused their son's death. That Joe was dead was news to them, they hadn't heard from him since they moved to Nevada a few years ago. They didn't know he'd moved to California; they didn't know he'd changed his name to Giuseppe Brandetti.

Al told them he would pay the cost of the lawyer and so forth. They stood to get as much as $5,000. He took them to a notary in Reno where they signed a whole bunch of papers and he gave them a thousand dollars. He said he'd mail copies of the papers to them, but they hadn't arrived yet. On the way to Reno, he'd bought them dinner at Al's and Sal's.

Emma and Tyler each ordered apple pie with ice cream and a milkshake for dessert. Emma had a cup of coffee.

It wasn't until the ride home when Tyler thought to ask, "Say, what's all this lawsuit stuff to you?"

"Oh, I'm just part of the legal process. You know, when a suit is filed in California from out of state, we have to check things out." She did not say who "we" were.

That and the five one-hundred-dollar bills she gave them seemed to satisfy their curiosity.

Chapter 27

"Sam Jones's attorney and I met with opposing counsel," Annie said. "The stated purpose of the meeting was to see if we could agree on a settlement."

"Mike doesn't want to settle," Lisa said, "but I'm not so sure."

"I know. But what our side wanted out of the meeting was to get a sense of their evidence. In order to try to get us to settle, they need to persuade us they have a strong case."

"Okay. But you suggested I come without Mike," Lisa said. "Why?"

"I thought it might be better. You know I love you both, so this is hard. What we have to discuss is pretty sensitive."

Lisa felt anxious. She didn't know what to do with her hands. She decided to take a sip of water to try to settle down. "Well, it works out better, anyway. Mike's doing a CNBC interview today."

"Here's what's happened," Annie said. "Opposing counsel subpoenaed emails, text messages and calendars from you, Mike and Jones. That was no surprise, since they claim you and Jones had a relationship; they're fishing for evidence of that. It seems all three of you keep very detailed electronic calendars and never delete anything.

What they discovered were three separate occasions when Jones was at an event you ran."

Before they bought the winery and she became general manager, Lisa had her own business as an event planner, mainly for fund raising events for local non-profit organizations. She was known then as the "Wine and Cheese Queen of Silicon Valley."

Annie handed Lisa a sheet of paper with the dates and details of the events.

"These are all when Mike was CEO of Attagenics," Lisa said anxiously, "and was commuting to Pasadena."

"And he was in Pasadena on each of those dates," Annie said, finishing the thought that was taking form in Lisa's head.

It took Lisa a moment to absorb this. "Each of those events probably had a hundred or more people at them. I don't even remember seeing Sam before the shooting, never mind meeting him," she said, shaking her head.

"Well, that was the part I wanted to tell you alone," Annie said.

"Just in case..."

Annie sighed. "Yes, just in case."

Lisa looked off in the distance for a bit, then seemed to snap out of her reverie. "It's all nonsense," she said grimly. "Complete and utter nonsense. So what else do they have and where do we stand?"

"They have these three events where you could have met. They'll characterize them as liaisons when your husband was out of town. They have you at the barn when the shooting took place. They'll claim you were already there when the shooting started. They have Jones staying in your home at the winery for a few weeks, with you there a good deal of the time.

"They're also trying to make something of your friendship with Sheriff Ryder. Him following your ambulance and waiting for Mike at the hospital instead of staying at the scene. Not letting you be interviewed by the detective until the next day. Getting guards posted outside Jones's room. Getting you in to see Jones at the hospital when there were strict no visitor orders. All circumstantial evidence of favoritism. They'll claim you used your influence on Sheriff Ryder to get him to back up the version of the shooting events that you and Jones gave."

"That sounds like a lot of evidence," Lisa said.

"If we go to trial, I'm pretty sure we can shred their evidence. It's all circumstantial. Still, in a civil case, they only need to convince nine of the twelve jurors to prevail. And the standard is 'a preponderance of the evidence' not 'beyond a reasonable doubt.' That means the jury will be instructed that if it's more than 50% likely that the charges are true, they're supposed to vote in the plaintiff's favor."

Lisa just shook her head. *How had it come to this?*

"That's why most civil suits are settled out of court," Annie said. "The legal costs, nuisance and uncertainty lead innocent parties to settle."

Lisa was too shell-shocked to say anything.

"If you want me to settle this, I'm certain we can. But I have another idea for you to consider.

"The lawyer for the other side, Ralph Farman, is the same guy who represented Brandetti in his dealings with

Jones. He runs a one-horse law office out of a hole-in-the-wall above a tattoo parlor in a part of downtown Napa that redevelopment hasn't quite reached.

"I got a copy of the claims against Brandetti's estate. Farman is claiming nearly $20,000 in unpaid legal bills. He's unlikely to see any of that. I think this lawsuit is his way of trying to recoup his loses.

"As for the Brandets, they haven't filed a tax return for several years. They live in the middle of nowhere in Nevada and seem to barely subsist on welfare and food stamps. They can't be paying Farman anything. I'm sure he's taken it on contingency.

"So what I want to do is escalate Farman's costs. We bury him in paper—subpoenas, motions, depositions. Show him if he presses on, we'll suck up his time and drag things out forever. I think he'll get his clients to drop the suit."

Two hours later, Annie received a text message from Lisa:

```
Talked to Mike.
Yes.
Escalate his costs.
Bury him.
```

Chapter 28

"Let's work on that tiger dream," she said.

It was Friday, and Lisa was at her third session with this new therapist. She'd starting seeing her a week ago, after she'd left the winery when she was served with the lawsuit.

She turned the lights out and closed the curtain on the office window. "Now close your eyes and just pay attention to your breathing."

Lisa did so. She felt herself relaxing.

"I want you to get back into the dream. When you're there, tell me. But keep your eyes closed."

After a few deep breaths, Lisa said, "Okay, I'm in the dream."

"Where are you?"

"I'm in my bed."

"What do you see?"

"Just the bed. I don't see anything past the edges of the mattress. It's sort of cloudy."

"Describe the bed."

"It's small. A child's bed. A white wooden headboard. There's a little pillow with a yellow pillowcase. The bottom sheet is white. The top sheet is yellow, and there's a yellow blanket."

"How old are you?"

"I'm just a child," Lisa said, her voice becoming a bit higher and softer. "I'm six years old."

"Look up. What do you see?"

"Nothing. It's sort of like I'm in a cloud."

"You and the bed."

"Yes."

"Look down over the side."

"No!" Lisa said, in a stubborn, little girl voice.

"Why not?"

"The tiger's down there. Under my bed."

"How do you know?"

"I hear him breathing. It's almost a growl."

"How do you feel?"

"I'm scared."

"What are you afraid of?"

"The tiger."

A pause, "I want to talk to the tiger. I want you to give the tiger a voice."

"Okay," Lisa said hesitantly, still in a little girl voice.

"Tiger, what are you doing under Lisa's bed?"

"I'm protecting her," Lisa said, in a deep voice. She felt surprised.

"What are you protecting her from, tiger?"

"Bad people."

"Are bad people there now?"

"Not right now. If there were, I'd be roaring at them."

"Lisa, is there anything you want to say to the tiger?"

"Tiger, you frighten me."

"What does the tiger answer?"

"You don't need to be afraid of me. I can't hurt you. I protect you."

"Lisa, I want you to try something. Have the tiger say, 'Lisa, I'm a part of you.'"

"Okay...Lisa, I'm a part of you."

"How does that feel?"

Lisa nodded. "It feels right." Lisa opened her eyes. "Oh my god," she said.

We were sitting at a small table with a white table cloth, looking out at the Pacific Ocean from our suite at the Ritz-Carlton. The cloudless sky was on fire as the sun set, a riot of reds and oranges.

The room service waiter had just laid out our meal and poured our first glass of wine. Now we were alone. I raised my wineglass. "To us," I said. "I love you."

Lisa raised her glass and clinked it with mine. "And I love you."

We had agreed that, at least for a while, weekends were sacrosanct. No business. No social engagements. No guests to entertain. Not even our grandson. We were going to go away and just be together. This weekend, it was Half Moon Bay, an isolated, picturesque little coastal village protected from the rest of densely populated San Mateo County by a mountain range, forests and farms.

As we started on our appetizers—a shrimp cocktail with extra cocktail sauce for me, a caprese salad for her—Lisa told me about her therapy session. She was excited and animated, which delighted me.

"So, you see, the tiger is part of me. It's the part that I need to use to protect myself from the bad guys when there's no one else to protect me."

"But you're always scared of the tiger in your dream," I said.

"Little girls aren't supposed to have tigers, Mike. My mother always scolded me if I raised my voice or got in a fight."

"I guess little boys are assumed to be tigers."

"Well, no one freaks out if boys show aggression sometimes. We didn't with our boys, and we won't with Brian."

"I guess most girls don't get to practice how to handle their aggression," I said.

"I didn't. I was supposed to stifle it."

"So you need to get to know your tiger," I said.

"Yes," she said, "and how to use it."

Chapter 29

General Durant sat in the back seat of the staff car as it motored south on Route 1 from Alexandria, Virginia to Army Intelligence Headquarters at Fort Belvoir. He'd just spent over an hour getting a full report from his operative about the Brandets. They'd met at a little coffee shop that had tables spaced well apart on a shaded patio.

As the number two officer in the entire Army intelligence apparatus, he had legions of personnel all over the world he could tap for missions. Yet the most valuable were the small number who appeared on no organization chart. They worked alone or in very small units. They were referred to as the Ghosts. They reported directly to him.

These were the anonymous men and women who would do whatever needed to be done, wherever it needed to be done. They never asked "why." They only asked "what" and, on occasion, "how." Though usually the ""how" was up to them.

Her report was thorough and detailed. Oral, of course. Nothing a Ghost did was ever written down, nor were their orders.

When she was done, they ordered second cups of coffee. She waited patiently, silently, while he thought. He reminded himself of the objectives: end the lawsuit and be sure the Brandets never poked their noses into Sam Jones's life again.

The first would be easy to achieve. Once done, the second could be accomplished by just killing the Brandets and disappearing their bodies. It was neat and clean, and dead men told no tales.

He considered an alternative he'd used before: drop them in a third world country, arrange for them to get a monthly cash payment on condition that they stay put and keep their mouths shut, and put them on the no-fly list to be sure they never returned. Tell them this was for their benefit, because the bad guys who killed their son were now after them because of the suit. This is what he would do if he thought he might need them again sometime.

But it didn't take long to convince himself that he wouldn't need those pathetic bozos again.

The Ghost was greeted warmly when she returned to the silver trailer. Off they went in her car to Reno, where the Brandets sat with her in an attorney's office. The Brandets dutifully signed more papers. What they signed fired Ralph Farman, retained their new Nevada attorney, and affirmed their desire to have the lawsuit against Lisa Gold and Sam Jones dropped.

She'd seen to it that they thought they were signing documents needed for them to get the money due them from the lawsuit she told them they had won. The Nevada lawyer was not part of that conversation.

Their legal chores completed, she took the Brandets out to a decent Reno steakhouse, where she allowed herself to chow down as they did, making sure that their beers kept coming. She then drove them home, assuring them that she'd be returning with their $5,000 just as soon as the papers they had signed were filed in California.

It was dark by the time they arrived at the trailer. As the Brandets staggered to their front door, she quietly followed. Just as Tyler was reaching for the door handle, the Ghost drew her silenced pistol and put two bullets into the backs of their heads.

She signaled her fellow Ghosts with her military-issued cell phone. It was an Android phone, but in addition to cellular and Wi-Fi, it was able to use the military satellite network. Twenty minutes later, the unmarked eighteen wheeler pulled up.

She worked quickly and efficiently with the four men on her team for this mission. The bodies were zipped into body bags and loaded into the truck. Next the old pickup truck was driven up ramps and secured onboard. Then the trailer was pulled in with a winch. The lawn chairs and a few other odds and ends were tossed in, and the area was policed and raked smooth with lawn rakes. From the time the truck arrived, the entire operation had taken eighteen minutes.

While all this activity was going on, the dog yapped excitedly and accepted an occasional pet. They had no orders about the dog, but felt kindly toward him, as he had the good judgement not to seem to miss the Brandets. They quickly agreed that she would drop him at an animal rescue shelter.

As she drove off with the dog, she ticked off her mental checklist. The Reno lawyer would kill the lawsuit tomorrow. The trailer and truck were headed for a junkyard in Lovelock. Then the bodies would be taken to a funeral home in Winnemucca, where they would be anonymously cremated. Both were a few hours east on I-80. After getting a good night's sleep at a motel, she would drop off the dog at the humane society in Truckee, just over the Nevada-California border off I-80 west,

The Brandets and all their worldly possessions had vanished without a trace. There was no evidence they had ever been there.

Chapter 30

Ralph Farman wasn't sure whether to be pissed off or relieved.

He'd just received notice that he had been fired by the Brandets and that their lawsuit had been dropped by their new Reno lawyer. There was also a check made out to him from the Reno lawyer's office for $2,500.

He was pissed off because he knew he'd never see the nearly $20,000 Brandetti had owed him when he died. He'd also been counting his cut of the multi-million dollar settlement Alvin Baxter had convinced them they'd get from Lisa Gold and Sam Jones.

When Baxter came to him, they'd quickly cut a deal. Baxter would pay him $2,000 to file the suit. Baxter would get the Brandets to sign whatever paperwork Farman needed. Farman would include documents giving Baxter their powers-of-attorney to open a bank account on their behalf. Baxter would add signature cards from the bank. He'd also be on the account and sign the signature card.

Farman knew what Baxter was doing. He would have the settlement check made out to the Brandets deposited in the bank account, then abscond with the money. The Brandets would never even know about the settlement.

Maybe Baxter would promise them a few bucks to sign all the papers, maybe he'd even pay them something from the settlement, but they'd get peanuts and Baxter would get millions.

And Farman would get one-third. He'd figured those rich suckers would gladly settle to get rid of the scandalous nuisance. He figured they'd negotiate down from the 20 million dollars to maybe 15 million. He'd been daydreaming about what he'd do with his five million dollar cut.

So he was pissed about that. But he was hugely relieved to get out from under the paper blizzard that Lisa Gold's and Sam Jones's attorneys had sent his way. How, he marveled, did they crank this stuff out? It just kept coming, day after day. And then there were the time consuming depositions. Those lawyers were deposing everyone under the sun. Farman felt like a puppet, jigging around as opposing counsel pulled his strings.

He should never have bought in to Baxter's dumbass scheme. The guy even said he had gotten the idea for the suit from a TV show, of all things. *I'm the lawyer, dammit. I should've known better.*

It was time to put this whole sorry Brandetti thing behind him.

Chapter 31

Lisa and I were already seated when Sam Jones arrived at Aldo's Café. Aldo's was the nearest thing we'd found in Los Gatos to the kind of little neighborhood restaurants we'd found in Italy, where the staff know your name, what you like to eat, how you like it prepared, and what wine you prefer with it.

Lisa caught Sam's eye and waved. As he approached the table, I stood and extended my hand. He shook hands tentatively. I gave him my macho man grip.

As we sat down, I said, "So you're the guy who's been running around with my wife."

Jones blanched. Lisa glared at me. "I'm kidding," I said.

"Mike, that was just awful," Lisa said.

"I'm sorry," I said, knowing we both knew I wasn't.

"It's okay," Jones said with a sheepish grin. "It sure broke the ice."

We already had a bottle of red and a bottle of white at the table. I asked Jones his preference, then poured him a glass of the Pinot Grigio.

"What better way to celebrate the end of this lawsuit drama than with good Italian food, wine, and some good company?" I said.

We all clinked glasses. I could tell Lisa was ready to forgive my rascally humor. We then gave another toast to our lawyers, whose clever maneuvers we were sure had led Farman and the Brandets to abandon the lawsuit.

It turned out that Jones and I were like two heavenly bodies orbiting the same sun but never coming into view of each other. We knew a lot of the same tech industry people. Lisa seemed pleased as we swapped stories.

By the end of the evening, I had to agree with her. Sam Jones was a nice guy.

As we drove home, Lisa said, "You know there could never have been anything between Sam and me."

"Of course," I said.

"No, I mean there *really* couldn't have been."

"Huh?"

"Mike, Sam's gay."

"He is?"

"Sometime you are so oblivious," she said. But she was smiling.

Chapter 32

Alvin Baxter couldn't believe his eyes. He'd driven around the area several times to be sure, and he was now certain this was where the trailer had been. There wasn't a trace of the Brandets. The lady at the post office hadn't seen them for a while, but, she said, she rarely did.

He figured that Jones and the Gold woman had probably just paid them off and who knew where they'd gone. Regardless, that bright idea of his for the lawsuit was clearly a dead-end. It was time to stop being so damn clever.

Baxter decided to spend the night in Reno. He skipped the gambling—hell, he was as close to broke as he'd ever been since he got out of the Army stockade. He got himself a cheap motel room, a pizza and a cold six-pack. It was time to take stock.

As he looked back over the last 10 years, he realized his life had been sort of suspended because of the money he'd stolen in Iraq and the double-cross by Adrian Hightower. He was sort of paralyzed, waiting for what was rightfully his.

With a dishonorable discharge and his hip injury in prison—it wasn't even enough to qualify as a limp—the career he'd planned in law enforcement would never be. So he'd had a series of low-paying security jobs for outfits that didn't do much of a background check. He'd work a while as a rent-a-cop, move to a different city, repeat. He'd been all over the Midwest, waiting. Waiting for what, he wondered now. Did he expect Hightower to appear out of the blue and hand him 9 million bucks?

When he'd recognized that Sam Jones was Adrian Hightower, he'd puzzled about how to get his money out of him. He worried that if he went after Jones, Jones would return the favor. Jones had plenty of resources to throw at the effort. Alvin had just a few thousand dollars and no friends, just a burning passion to get what was due him, and maybe some revenge while he was at it.

As he got to his fourth beer, he decided that he had to focus on the money. It was the money that would change his life. Revenge might be sweet, but he was pretty sure the pleasure it would bring would fade.

Which got him to thinking about really changing his life. If he could get that money, he could establish a new identity like Hightower had. Then Jones would never find him. In fact, if he changed his identity first and made Alvin Baxter disappear, he could go after Jones without worrying about Jones coming back at him.

Baxter had figured that Hightower became Jones in order to hide from him. Then when his picture got plastered all over after the shooting in the vineyard, he must have called in some favors with Army brass to get his hospital room guarded. Maybe Hightower had used some of Baxter's cash to bribe one or more of them back when he'd gotten him court-martialed and ripped him off.

Over the fifth beer, he ruminated about his big mistake. After Jones left the hospital, he'd called the Napa Sheriff's Department and asked to speak to the guard he'd met outside Jones's room. He'd gotten the name of the guard off of his name tag. He was told there was no such person in the department. This confirmed his suspicion that the guy was really military. He'd been nervous because he realized that when he'd used Wayne to chat with the guard at the hospital, he'd let the guard get a good, long look at his own face. If they were protecting Jones from Baxter, surely they'd have shown the guard his photo. But the guard showed no sign of recognizing him. That was a worrisome loose end.

Then beer logic took over. Maybe they hadn't shown the guard his picture. Maybe he no longer looked much like the picture they had—he was sure heavier and had longer hair than when he was in Iraq. Maybe the guard was just a dufus. He remembered what he'd seen on a lot of TV crime shows: there were always loose ends. He decided to let it go, and enjoy that sixth beer.

Chapter 33

Friday morning, Baxter called the security company he worked for and told his boss he was fully recovered and would be back to work on Monday.

His boss was fine with that. Rent-a-cops were famous for not showing up for work, going on benders, and just plain disappearing. That Baxter had called in sick in advance of his shift and then kept him posted on the progress of whatever ailed him—Baxter had never told him exactly what that was and he'd never asked—was good enough for him.

He was in the warm body business. He had a few simple requirements for his employees. Show up for work on time. Stay awake. Stay sober. Don't steal anything. Call 9-1-1 in case anything weird happens. By this standard, Baxter made the grade.

Baxter drove from Reno to his hovel in Gary, Indiana. He arrived for his night shift Monday at the reprocessed auto parts plant. Thursday night, he made his move.

The plant used to be a steel plant in Gary's heyday. As the steel industry had moved offshore over the last 50 years, Gary had crumbled. Its population was less than half of what it had been at its peak in the '60s. Buildings of every kind were boarded up and abandoned. The cavernous plant was now a hub for stripping down old or wrecked vehicles, salvaging useful parts, and distributing them throughout the Midwest. It was also the biggest chop shop operation for 500 miles. The authorities ignored that aspect of the business; it was one of the largest employers and property tax payers left in Gary.

Baxter knew they had a lot of cash in the safe Thursday night. Friday was payday, and the plant employed dozens of off-the-books workers, mostly Spanish-speaking, who were paid in cash. They also always had cash on hand to pay for vehicles of questionable ownership that showed up regularly, when paperwork and a paper trail were undesirable.

Baxter was no safe cracker. He used a pneumatic wrench to remove the big bolts that fastened the safe to the concrete office floor. Then he drove a forklift through the wall of the office—it was flimsy, built out on the plant floor with two-by-fours and sheetrock—and used it to load the heavy safe onto a trailer. The wrench, forklift and trailer were all readily available in the plant.

He loaded an oxy-acetylene torch, fuel tank and mask onto the trailer and covered it with a tarp. When he was satisfied that the tarp was secure, he opened one of the overhead doors, and drove his car onto the plant floor. When the trailer was hitched, he was off. Baxter figured he had a good four or five hours before his theft was discovered. By that time, he'd be a couple of hundred miles away, at a cabin he'd rented in a heavily wooded area near Davenport, Iowa, patiently cutting open the safe.

As he drove west, Baxter felt exhilarated. It was as if he'd been hibernating since Iraq, and had just awakened.

He was astonished at how easy disappearing would be. All his worldly belonging worth taking were in his one suitcase. Some clothes, toiletries and not much else. He'd already tossed his cheap cell phone. His skinny wallet contained an ATM card, a bank credit card and driver's license, along with the six-hundred or so dollars in cash— he'd drained his account with a few visits to the ATM during the last few days. So when the driver's license and two plastic cards were destroyed, Alvin Baxter would no longer exist.

Oh, yeah, he also needed to ditch the nearly worthless car.

The police found the submerged car in the Mississippi River north of Davenport. The driver had missed the bend in the road and gone through the guardrail and over the embankment. The front windows and driver's-side door were open, and the driver's body was never found. The assumption was that it had been swept away downstream.

The license plate number was traced to an APB that had been issued by Indiana State Police for an Alvin Baxter. A few days later, they found the trailer, safe and equipment stolen from the Gary plant in a garage behind a rental vacation cabin just a few miles from the crash site. The rental agent had contacted the police when she found the garage open and the cabin vacant during a routine check.

The safe had been cut open. It stood empty. There were a couple of empty whiskey bottles in the garage and the empty cans from of a six-pack in the cabin. A drunk Alvin Baxter had obviously sped off to his death with the money from the safe. It had probably floated down the Mississippi along with his body. That completed the picture for the police.

Chapter 34

"Tell me a bit about yourself, Wayne."

Lisa and Wayne were in the tasting room. They were facing each other, sitting on stools at the tasting bar. It was just after 9:00 a.m. and the room wasn't open to the public until 10:00 a.m. The tasting room staff would start arriving in a half an hour.

"Not much to tell," Wayne said. "Got out of high school in L.A. in 1950 and was drafted into the Army. Served in Korea. I liked Army life. Retired after 40 years of service."

"What did you do after the Army?"

"Went back to L.A. Got a job for the park's department supervising groundskeepers. Retired from that after 20 years in 2010."

"So you're a double-dipper?"

"That I am," he said proudly. "Got an Army pension and a city pension."

"Family?"

"Wife died in 2008. Cancer. We'd been married 53 years."

"Children?"

"Nope. Army keeps you moving around too much. We didn't think it was a good life for kids."

"I understand you live at the Veterans Home."

"Yeah. Moved up here after I retired from the park's department. I'm in independent living. Got great healthcare, and I'm around other military old fogeys."

"José wants you to work here in the tasting room part time."

"Yeah, well, I been coming here two, three times a week for a while, just tasting wine and schmoozing for a couple hours. Kinda my day camp."

"Well, José will schedule your hours. It's an hourly job, no benefits."

"I don't need benefits, and it's not about the money. It's about having interesting folks to talk to. And I'm learning a bit about wine."

"Well, I look forward to having you here at Duncan Gold," Lisa said, smiling and offering her hand.

Good people, thought Wayne. Lisa Gold, Sam Jones, the tasting room folks, they were good people. Treated him like a person, like he still had value. Not like Baxter, who had dropped him like a used up old relic without even a thank you.

Lisa took off in her single-engine Cessna 172 Skyhawk from Napa County Airport just before 5:00 p.m. The route south to San Jose kept her over I-680 most of the way, and she always felt a bit smug watching the bumper-to-bumper traffic below as commuters headed home.

It was an up-and-down flight, meaning that by the time she got to her cruising altitude of 6,000 feet she only had a few minutes to relax before starting her descent. Just before she reached altitude, she heard a strange beeping sound. She checked all her instruments. Everything appeared normal. Then she realized the sound was coming from behind her.

Lisa fumbled around and found a cardboard shoebox wedged under the backseat. She yanked it out and placed it next to her on the front passenger seat. She removed the top and found a small device that she later learned was a handheld altimeter, programmed to beep at 5,500 feet. Only later did it occur to her that it could have triggered a bomb.

Under the device, she found a piece of plain white paper. There was a handwritten message printed in large capital letters:

```
BOOM!
WE CAN GET TO YOU ANYWHERE.
ASK YOUR BOYFRIEND.
```

Sam Jones sorted through the day's mail. Buried in the junk mail that he didn't even bother opening was a postcard with a picture of the Eiffel Tower. On the other side was a handwritten message printed in capital letters:

```
ADRIAN
10,000,000
```

That evening, Lisa, Amy Wu and I sat at our breakfast room table. Lisa had called me and then Amy as soon as she'd landed in San Jose. The box and its contents were on the table.

"We'll check everything for prints, but I don't expect to find any," Amy said.

"Except mine," Lisa said.

"Okay, but who has access to the plane?"

"It's parked outside the hanger with other private planes," Lisa said. "There aren't crowds, but all sorts of people come and go, and there isn't that much security."

"Who do you think this 'boyfriend' is?"

"My guess is Sam Jones." Amy had been there at the start of the whole Sam Jones adventure, when I'd first heard about the vineyard shooting. Lisa brought her up-to-date, right up to when the lawsuit was dropped.

Amy looked at me, seemed to hesitate, then asked Lisa, "Is there any relationship I need to know about?"

"None," Lisa said. "Though Mike and I have become sort of friends with Sam."

I nodded at that. "Where do we go from here?" I said.

"Do you want to get the police involved?"

"Not yet," I said.

"Why not?" Lisa said.

"They have different priorities than we do," I said firmly. "They won't believe what we tell them. They'll want to investigate everything, they'll assume all of us are lying to them, and they'll want to figure out what crimes have been committed, and who committed them. Our priorities are keeping you safe and putting an end to this nonsense."

Lisa looked taken aback by my outburst.

Amy looked at me, then Lisa. "Well, I suggest we meet with Sam as soon as possible. Meanwhile, I'll get some people to check over the plane thoroughly. Then I'll work out getting it secured in a hanger in San Jose and Napa. I recommend that you stay grounded for a while."

Lisa looked at me. I nodded. I wanted to tell her to hide with an army of bodyguards around her. But I realized I was steamrolling over her, so I kept that to myself.

"Okay, but this needs to get resolved fast," she said.

"Then I think we get you 24/7 bodyguard service, and have someone with you all the time."

"This better be over before the next time I go to the winery," Lisa said.

"It should be over soon," Amy said. "I'll get right on the security after we call Jones. Who makes that call?"

When Sam got the call, he said he'd be right over. It was a short but agonizing drive.

He had never told a soul about Baxter. Now, he was certain Baxter was after him, and, from what Lisa had told him on the phone, was using Lisa to get leverage. Baxter wanted the money.

No matter how he handled this, he was screwed. The only question was how he wanted to be screwed. By the time he walked to the Gold's front door, he had decided how he had to proceed.

Now four of us were at the breakfast room table. It was a different Sam Jones who sat there. His normal irrepressible cheerfulness had been replaced by a somber demeanor.

"You have no idea how sorry I am that you two have been dragged into this," Sam said, looking first at Lisa, then at me. "I had no idea that would happen. But I have to handle this very carefully.

"Someone is after me who wants some money from me. A good deal of money. I got confirmation of that today. I can't tell you more without incriminating myself and making all three of you witnesses who could be called to testify against me.

"So here is what I want to do. I want to get with my attorney tomorrow and get an investigator on the case, so I can fully disclose to them what I know and be protected by attorney-client privilege."

"You're right about that," Amy said. "There is no privilege with an investigator unless it's part of attorney work product."

"But…" I started to say.

"But in reality, most investigators have very poor memories," Amy said. "Unless we write stuff down or record it, we forget. I'm afraid I suffer from that faulty memory."

I looked at Lisa. She nodded. Then I looked at Sam. "Look, we've worked with Amy and her team for years on the faulty memory theory. Lisa and I have the same problem, it's a sort of amnesia."

Sam said nothing for a bit. "So you're saying I should trust you."

"We're saying you can trust us," Lisa said. "We've been in these sorts of situations before."

"But you have no idea what I'm going to tell you," he said.

"Okay," Lisa said. "If it's rape, child abuse or murder, keep it to yourself."

"None of the above," he said, with a sheepish grin.

"Then let's try this," I said. "You tell your story. If any of us thinks you're going out of our comfort zone, we'll stop you. Agreed?"

"So what I tell you tonight stays in this room?"

"Yes," I said.

Amy and Lisa nodded. "Yes," they said.

None of us had had any dinner, and it was probably going to be a long conversation. So while Sam composed himself, we ordered pizza from the Los Gatos MySlice. Lisa and I got everyone a soft drink. It was clearly an evening for clear heads.

Sam made eye contact with each of us in turn, then started in on his story.

"This goes back to the invasion of Iraq in 2003. When we took Baghdad, a soldier named Alvin Baxter was part of a unit that was tasked with guarding a truck loaded with cash Saddam Hussein was hoarding. He managed to steal 10 million dollars and kept it hidden in Abu Ghraib prison, where he was a guard.

"I was a CID investigator. That's Army intelligence. I was assigned to the Abu Ghraib case. Sergeant Baxter was one of the targets. During the investigation, I connected Baxter with the theft, which I had investigated at the time. I told him I knew he had stolen the money. He told me he still had it hidden in country and needed a way to get it home. The Army was obsessive about making sure no loot of any kind made it out of Iraq.

"I figured out a way to get the money into the States. I cut a deal with Baxter. I'd get a million dollars. I'd be sure he got off on the Abu Ghraib charges and would get his nine million.

"Instead, I made sure Baxter got court martialed. He was convicted. While he was in the stockade, I got the Army to send me home, discharge me, and relocate me with a new identity. That's how I got here. And I had the 10 million dollars. And Baxter couldn't find me when he finally got home."

The pizza arrived. The MySlice CEO got especially fast service. In any case, we took a break for the bathroom and to sort out plates and beverages and so forth.

When we were all settled back at the table, we started in on the pizza. I was surprised at how hungry I was. Before Sam could start in again, Amy had some questions.

"Why did the Army send you home and relocate you?"

"Well, not everyone was crazy about the Abu Ghraib case. Some thought the guards were just doing their duty, protecting America, and there were some pretty extreme views.

"The original whistleblower had faced hostility when he went home, so much that the Army relocated him. As the investigator, I was getting some grief while I was still in Iraq, including death threats. So I asked for the same thing."

"I remember the whistleblower," Amy said. "He went public. But you got a new identity."

"Well, those death threats had me freaked out, and I guess the Army didn't want anything to happen to me when I got home that would bring even more negative attention to the Abu Ghraib scandal."

"What was your name before you became Sam Jones?" Lisa said.

"Let me get something out of my car," Sam said.

He returned in a minute and showed us a postcard. "I got this in the mail today."

"Don't pick it up," Amy said. "Fingerprints." She got up and retrieved tweezers and a clear plastic bag from her purse. She used the tweezers to pick up the card, inserted it into the bag and sealed it. The she put it back on the table.

"It's the Eiffel Tower," Lisa said.

Holding the edge of the bag, Sam turned the card over.

```
ADRIAN
10,000,000
```

"I get the 10 million" I said. "Who's Adrian?"

"I was born Adrian Hightower."

Yes, dummy, I thought. *A high tower*. I decided to keep my keen sense of the obvious to myself.

"So we have the warning Lisa got today, and you got this," Amy said. "They're saying they know who you really are and that you have the stolen money. And they're threatening Lisa."

"You still have the money?" Lisa said.

"Let's just say it gave me my start as an investor here in the Valley," Sam said.

"Wait a minute," I said. I realized that Sam was not quite through with his story. This seemed to always happen when a presentation got interrupted. When you try to continue, you get sidetracked by questions about what you already presented. "Why don't we let Sam finish his story?"

"Almost done. So I'm here with 10 million dollars and a new identity. Baxter returns to the States but I'm nowhere to be found. About 10 years pass. No sign of Baxter. Then there's this shooting thing with Brandetti. The story with my picture is everywhere. Since Baxter last saw me, I've shaved my head and grown a beard. I really don't look much like I did 10 years ago. Still, I'm worried that Baxter will recognize me. So I get a guard posted outside my room with a vague story about feeling threatened."

"Because you couldn't reveal the real reason," Lisa said.

"Yeah. Anyway, time passes. Still no sign of Baxter. I figure I'm in the clear. Until today."

We all worked on our pizza awhile.

"No demands," Amy said. "He hasn't said what he wants from you yet."

"He wants the money," Sam said.

"Yes, but he hasn't given you any instructions. That should be the next step."

"Should I pay?" Sam said.

"You don't have to decide yet," Amy said. "But even if you pay, he knows about your crime. He can blackmail you forever."

"That's what I think, too," Sam said.

"One more thing," Amy said. "If Baxter knows Sam Jones is Adrian Hightower, you don't have to keep your old identity a secret anymore."

"I guess I don't have to, but I want to. I was glad to make a clean break from my family, and I'd rather not open old wounds. I also don't want the publicity that might come from the story."

"It also might spook Baxter," Amy said.

"The thing is, he can't hold that over my head. If it comes down to it, I can live with it coming out."

"If he reveals your help in stealing the money, he incriminates himself," I said. "So that's got to be a kind of last gasp move."

"You mean, if he does that, he can kiss the money good-bye?" Lisa said.

"Yeah, so it's really got to be another threat," I said, looking at my wife. "Like what that shoebox implied."

We all let that sink in.

"What if we go public and deny that we had any relationship." Sam said to Lisa. "Then Baxter will know threatening you won't work. That'll get you out of this mess."

"The thing is," Lisa said, "we didn't do that when the lawsuit was filed. We agreed to ignore it and not fuel the news media."

"Which worked," I said. "You think Baxter won't be fooled if we went public now?"

"Would you be, now that the lawsuit is gone? Why make a big deal about our non-relationship except to communicate with Baxter?"

Lisa was right. That ploy probably wouldn't work. In fact, it might just convince Baxter his approach was working.

We agreed that we needed to let Baxter make the next move.

We went over the exact steps we'd take to protect Lisa and Sam. When Sam left, after again apologizing profusely for dragging us into his problem, Amy grabbed a pen and notebook out of her purse and started writing intensely, while Lisa and I cleaned up from dinner.

Ten minutes later, the three of us were back at the table.

"I wanted to get his story down while it was fresh in my mind," Amy said. "If I took notes while he was here, he'd have freaked out."

"You think he was telling the truth?" Lisa said.

"Pretty much. But there are a couple of things that bother me. First, I buy the Army relocating him. While you were in the kitchen, I looked up Abu Ghraib on my phone and found mention of the whistleblower being relocated by the Army due to problems when he got home. But with Sam, they went a lot further, getting him a new identity. I don't think that's exactly something the Army usually does."

"Did you find Hightower's name online?" Lisa said.

"I did. But just that he was the Abu Ghraib investigator. No other information. That's no surprise. Investigators never get much mention. It isn't like TV or movies." Amy flashed her pixie smile. "We're unsung heroes."

"Maybe the identity change had something to do with Sam being in military intelligence," I said. "They probably deal with agents and false identities all the time."

"That could explain it," Amy said. "Who knows what else he was mixed up in? Maybe they wanted him to disappear for other reasons.

"Another thing that didn't ring true to me was why Sheriff Ryder put a guard on his hospital room. That's not exactly standard procedure. It's expensive. Not something I think they'd do just because he said he was nervous."

"I can ask Jeff Ryder about that," Lisa said. "I'll call him tomorrow."

"Okay, but don't tell him why you're asking," Amy said.

"I can do that."

In bed that night, I told Lisa how worried I was about her safety. We both remembered the last time we had a bodyguard here. That ended with Lisa being kidnapped and both of us almost being put through a woodchipper. I didn't want to think it, never mind say it, but I had visions of Baxter kidnapping Lisa and holding her for ransom.

"I'll promise to stay close to home for a while," Lisa said. "I'll be very careful."

We held hands in the dark awhile. "I'll let my tiger loose," Lisa said.

Amy Wu did not drive away from the Gold's house until the first of a series of security guards arrived. They would work in shifts. She briefed the guard and left him sitting on the front porch. Then she texted Lisa to let her know that she and the house were covered.

Sam had wanted to arrange for his own security, so Amy had given him the number of the security service. He had agreed to pay Kowalski-Wu investigations for their work on his case. After he left the Gold's, Lisa and Mike had added some assignments that Sam was unaware of, for which they would pay.

Chapter 35

Dirk Clark felt more alive than any time he could remember. The funk he'd been in since Adrian Hightower had ripped him off in Iraq was just a sad memory.

He was amazed at how easy it had been to get rid of Alvin Baxter. The mechanics of killing him off had gone remarkably smoothly, but what really surprised him was that he didn't miss old Alvin a bit.

He'd been astonished when he counted his haul from the safe. There was just over $100,000, double what he'd expected. He decided that was a sign that his luck had changed.

He'd chosen his new name carefully. He was a fan of Clive Cussler's Dirk Pitt character, and thought the name Dirk was ruggedly masculine. He also liked Tom Clancy's John Clark, and remembered reading somewhere that women were drawn to men whose names ending with the letter k. A double dose of that wouldn't hurt! The old man who sold him his new identity packet asked him if he was naming himself after Dick Clark. Dirk did not understand the question.

Where Alvin Baxter didn't have the patience to plan carefully, Dirk Clark, though a man of action, knew the value of thorough preparation. His new identity papers cost $15,000, but he was confident that the passport, driver's license and social security card were flawless. The deal even included a Visa and MasterCard with decent credit limits. When he did a credit check on Dirk Clark using his new social security number, he found he had an unremarkable but believable credit background and a decent FICO score.

Before he'd gotten the photos for his passport and driver's license, he had some cosmetic surgery. He'd chosen the "moderately chiseled" option. His cheekbones were padded, his jaw and chin squared off, and the skin around his eyes was smoothed. None of the individual changes was extreme, but the result was that he looked a lot less baby-faced and more like Brad Pitt.

He added blue contacts over his brown eyes, and got a short haircut. When he looked in the mirror, the guy who looked back was a stranger. But a handsome devil! Yes, once he had real money, Dirk Clark was going to be the chick magnet Alvin Baxter had only dreamed about.

Dirk holed up in a cheap motel off I-80, about 20 minutes east of the Napa exit. They accepted cash, probably actually preferred it, and he was being real careful about not using his credit card. It wasn't for nothing that he watched TV.

He spent days thinking through how to get his money from Sam Jones. A lot of that thinking was powered by Budweiser.

He was also distracted by the come-ons he was getting from women. The motel receptionist, the gal at the nearby 7-11, and the waitress at the nearby diner had all been easy scores. Hell, he needed a break from all the hard thinking he was doing. And it was about time his luck with chicks had changed. Too bad he hadn't thought of plastic surgery and contacts sooner.

He had made one pass at Sam Jones that had failed miserably, but he'd gotten a lot of useful intel and was determined to learn from his mistakes. One thing he had going for him was time. He still had plenty of money, and he figured Jones wasn't going anywhere.

He certainly didn't want 10 million bucks in cash. He painstakingly researched how to set up a foreign bank account whose ownership was obscured and then move the money to accounts of his own. That meant he wanted the funds wired.

So how to persuade Jones to do that?

Threatening to expose Jones wouldn't work. He had no real proof. Jones had only given him the vaguest idea of how he'd get the cash from Iraq to the States. And even if he did expose Jones, he could then kiss the money good-bye for sure.

He could have him beaten up, and let him know that the attacks would continue and get more severe until he wired the money. Maybe burn down his house, too.

He could kidnap Jones and refuse to release him until he forked over the money.

He could threaten or even kidnap someone Jones cared about and hold them for ransom. As best he could tell,

Jones had no close family, but he did have a relationship with Lisa Gold. She and her husband were really rich, which worried him a bit, because they could afford protection and would probably try to hunt him down ruthlessly. Actually kidnapping her would likely draw in the Feds, too. Not a good idea.

But maybe threats would be enough. And threats were a lot less risky than actual violence. He figured the cops were less likely to devote much effort to mere threats.

Maybe, he thought, he could get just threatening enough to get Jones to give in, without getting law enforcement too involved. Do a full-court-press of threats. The more he thought about that, the more appealing it was. And he could always escalate to more violence later if needed.

After 10 days, he decided he'd thought and planned enough. His head was aching, and he was getting claustrophobic. He needed to get out of there and get moving.

Where Alvin Baxter had been a morose, beaten-down loser, Dirk Clark was a winner, a man of bold yet thoughtful action. And he was ready to act. First, he'd fired a warning shot at Lisa Gold and Sam Jones. And that was just for starters.

Chapter 36

He knew he'd drunk too much, but knowing that and acting on it were very different things. He'd tried a less forceful approach, but that had gotten nowhere. It was time for a more direct attack.

A voice in the back of his mind urged patience and caution. But the front of his alcohol-inspired mind shouted, *Screw it*.

Oddly, given his paranoid reaction and 24/7 bodyguards after the shooting, Sam Jones had skimped on security. He'd just arranged for a bodyguard for 12 hours daily, during the daytime. He'd also upgraded his home security system. It now had live camera feeds when he was home. The cameras were monitored somewhere in the cloud—actually, it was in Bangalore, India—and, should anything look amiss, local law enforcement would be alerted. That was the extent of his new security measures.

His bodyguard had gone off duty at 8:00 p.m. Then Sam decided to go out and get some frozen yogurt. Thus he was alone as he pulled into his driveway that evening. The garage door opened smoothly as he pulled up and eased his BMW inside. As soon as the car stopped, he felt a sharp jolt. He glanced in the rearview mirror. The front of a very large SUV filled the mirror. He unbuckled and, as he began to open the car door, it was jerked out of his hands and he felt a blow on his head.

As Sam regained consciousness, he slowly assessed his situation. He could see faint light, but there was a bag of some sort over his head. His mouth was taped shut. His hands were secured behind his back. He was lying down in a cramped space and his legs were taped together, probably in more than one place. He was terrified.

He thought he was lying on the back seat of a car. This was confirmed as it became darker and the ride became bumpier.

After what seemed like forever but was probably just a few minutes, the vehicle stopped. He heard a door open, then another, and he was roughly pulled into a seated position.

"Listen to me carefully." The voice was vaguely familiar, the speech slow, as if the speaker were carefully choosing and enunciating each word. "You cheated me. You cheated my family. Now you must make it right. There will be no second chance. You have one week."

Sam was manhandled out of the car and fell helplessly to the ground. He felt the bonds on his wrists release. He struggled to his knees and pulled the pillowcase off of his head just in time to see the big, silver Chevy Tahoe speed away through the woods.

He frantically tore the duct tape off his face and unwrapped his knees and ankles. He got to his feet, then bent over and vomited.

Sam's cell phone had no reception. He walked through the redwoods along the dirt trail the Tahoe had taken. Soon he came to a winding, one-lane mountain road. He was pretty sure he'd felt the car make a right onto the dirt road, so he made a left. After perhaps a mile, he came to a clearing, his cell phone grabbed a bar's worth of cellular service, and he opened his Uber app and hailed a ride. Watching the dot that showed the progress of the Uber driver toward him was remarkably reassuring.

When he got home, the first thing he did, even before he rinsed the stale vomit from his mouth, was call and arrange for 24/7 bodyguard service.

Chapter 37

Amy Wu liked to keep a professional distance from her clients. It was okay to be empathetic when the situation called for it, but if you got emotionally involved, you'd soon burn out.

Lisa and Mike Gold were exceptions. Her long and complicated history with them made it impossible for her to be anything but emotionally involved. They had become like family.

They'd first met years ago when Barry Samson asked Mike to start a company to develop the next generation of technology for Forward Data Systems, where Samson was founder and CEO. For a variety of reasons, Samson had been unable to get his behemoth enterprise to do the job. Samson, who trusted no one, secretly planted Amy, an industrial espionage pro, on Mike's staff to spy on him. Samson also had her set up a paper trail that he could use, if needed, to threaten Mike with being charged with embezzlement if he didn't kowtow to Samson on command.

Mike had unraveled that whole scheme after Samson was killed. Amy had split to L.A. to hide out and avoid the fallout. She always smiled to herself when she remembered

Don Vito Cangelosi's two goons showing up and persuading her to call Mike and confess her sins. Those thugs had scared the crap out of her!

Mike had forgiven those sins. Later, he had connected Amy with Curt Kowalski, who became her partner at Kowalski-Wu Investigations after she'd "gone straight" and gotten her private investigator's license. Since then she had been involved in a number of cases with Lisa and Mike, some business, some personal.

So when she arrived at her office the next morning, the first thing she did was read the overnight messages from her staff and start sending them assignments for the day. An hour later, she had cleared the deck to focus on the Gold-Jones case.

Amy had taken Sam's frantic call the night before. Once she heard that he was okay and had finally taken his personal security more seriously, she reassured him that she would have a dossier on Mr. Baxter very soon.

She had him repeat what Baxter said to him very carefully. She copied it down verbatim, then read it back to him. He made a few minor corrections, then repeated the process. She wanted to get the exact wording while Sam's memory of it was fresh.

She'd asked Sam if he recognized Baxter's voice. He said it sounded vaguely familiar, but after 10 years he had no real memory of how Baxter had sounded.

She probed for anything he could recall about the SUV. It wasn't much, and, unlike on TV, no one seemed to ever get a license plate number. Sam was no exception.

After finishing the call with Sam, she called Lisa's security detail and passed on the information about Sam's little adventure.

Now she called in her lead researcher and got her working on Baxter. Then she turned her attention to Sam Jones. Lisa and Mike had decided it was time to do a deep dive into his background. She wiggled her fingers like a pianist warming up for a solo recital, and plunged into both open and supposedly secure databases. By noon, she had wrung the sponge dry.

As expected, there was no Sam Jones until his arrival in San Jose a decade earlier. He'd initially lived in a rented condo, then bought his current home in Los Gatos for cash just after the financial crisis hit and the bottom fell out of the real estate market.

Except for one exception, Sam's business career was also as expected. After his first year in the Valley, he began investing in tech startups, providing seed money. These angel investments never exceeded $250,000 and were often for much less. Like most angels, he lost his entire investment on most deals as the startups went belly-up. But his occasional wins more than made up for his loses. His disastrous plunge into winemaking with Brandetti had dented his net worth, but she figured it was still about 15 million dollars.

He had no criminal record. In addition to his legal dustup with Brandetti, he'd been involved in a few lawsuits, the kind investors typically get into. None had amounted to much, and they had all been resolved.

His personal life seemed unremarkable. He was a minor philanthropist, serving on the boards for several local nonprofits over the years. No marriages. Not a known gambler. Modest spending habits for someone with his wealth.

The glaring exception to what she'd expected to find in Sam's background was a company named Norcal Cash Services he had started soon after arriving in San Jose. Norcal had quickly acquired five mom-and-pop check cashing and payday loan shops. As soon as she came across that, she knew how Sam had laundered the 10 million dollars in cash. She saw that he had patiently pumped that money through this cash-intensive business over the years. Norcal Cash Services had been sold earlier in the year to a Julio Trevino. She surmised that Sam no longer needed its services.

Amy reheated a burrito she had stashed in the break room refrigerator, grabbed a bottle of Fuze, and took her lunch back to her desk.

She turned her internet search to Adrian Hightower. He was the only son of a wealthy Newport, Rhode Island family. Very old money. He'd dropped out of Yale in his freshman year and enlisted in the Army. Amy thought that that couldn't have pleased the family. His parents were still alive and active in Newport society. He had one sister who had married within the family's social circle and dropped off the radar.

She found the story of Saddam Hussein's cash hoard had been reported by several news outlets online. It was as Sam had said, about 130 million was never recovered and was assumed to have fallen into the hands of Iraqi insurgents.

After he was discharged from the Army, she could find nothing further about him. Adrian Hightower had vanished. If his family had attempted to find him, they had done it very discretely. Of course, it was possible that they knew where he was but had broken with him after the Yale debacle. Or still had contact with him but kept it to themselves.

Amy was contemplating the ways of wealthy patrician families when her researcher popped in and said she was ready to report on Alvin Baxter.

Except for the last few weeks, it was a boring report. Baxter had been an almost invisible person. There was barely any evidence online that he had existed before he enlisted in the Army. He was one of the court martialed Abu Ghraib guards, served an eight-month sentence and was given a dishonorable discharge.

Baxter then drifted from one mid-west city to another. His employment was spotty the first year or so, then became more regular. He mostly worked as a security guard, never earning more than $40,000 in a year, and often a lot less. There were a couple of DUIs that first year, then nothing but the occasional traffic ticket.

Then a few weeks ago, things got exciting. According to police reports, Baxter had stolen a safe from the plant in Gary, Indiana where he was night watchman. The safe was later found cut open in the garage of a cabin somewhere in Iowa. Baxter's car had been found in the Mississippi River. Police concluded he had driven through a guard rail while drunk. His body and the estimated $100,000 in cash had never been found, presumably swept downstream.

"Family?" Amy said.

"I dug hard for it, like you asked. Single mom. No evidence of a father. No siblings. Mom died in an auto accident just before he enlisted. Might have been why he did. No record of marriages. All tax returns filed as single."

"So no evidence of a family," Amy said.

"Nope."

"What about the shoebox and postcard?"

"No prints on the postcard except Jones's. The card itself is from a major supplier, and can even be purchased online. You have to buy a pack of them, but they're cheap. Postmark is the San Jose Meridian Avenue post office."

"So a dead end."

"I guess so. Same for the shoebox and note. Only Lisa Gold's prints. Generic shoebox you can buy lots of places, including online. The note is on common plain white paper. The one thing is that the printing looks like it was done by the same person."

Amy sighed. *Where's a clue when you need it?* She thought.

"Anything else on this?"

"No, that's it for now. Nice job."

Sam's abductor's note said Sam had cheated his family. Baxter had no family. Was that just a red herring? Or a clue? Amy couldn't figure out what to do with the contradiction, so she just tucked it away for the time being.

Baxter also had still made no demand. She was pretty sure that would be his next move.

Chapter 38

Sam received the text message at about the same time Amy was contemplating Baxter's next move.

```
10 million
Will send wire instructions in 24 hours
Wire right away
Or pay the price
```

"It was from a burner phone," Amy said. "No way to trace it."

We were again meeting at our house. It was late afternoon. Amy had arrived a bit before Sam was scheduled to show up, and had briefed Lisa and me on the day's developments.

When Sam arrived, we kicked around the pros and cons of paying. We also reviewed the option of going to the police.

"So what do you want to do, Sam?" Amy said.

"I don't want cops. And I don't think paying will be the end of the extortion."

"So we just sit tight and wait for his reaction." I said.

"I wonder why the change in schedule," Amy said.

"What change?" Sam said.

Amy flipped through her notebook, then read, "'You have one week.' Isn't that what he said when he took you?"

"You're right, he did."

"Maybe he's getting antsy," I said.

"Maybe. In any case, I think we both ought to double-down on your security details," Amy said. She got no pushback on that.

Lisa hung back as Mike and Sam left Amy's office. She lowered her voice and said, "I called Jeff Ryder and asked about those guards on Sam's hospital room. He said he was sorry but he could not tell me anything about that. He's never been tight-lipped like that before."

Amy had no idea if that was important or not. She just jotted it down in her notebook, where all such loose threads resided.

Ralph Farman was a bit distracted as he left his office that evening. It was late, he hadn't had dinner and was thinking of a nice juicy burrito grande.

He was also irked that his new client had blown off their meeting. It had been an odd call. The caller first asked if he knew Alvin Baxter. When he said he did, the caller said Baxter had recommended Farman as someone who could handle a thorny legal problem. Would Farman be able to meet that evening? Would he accept a personal check as a retainer?

Retainer was a magic word for Farman who was still berating himself about the Brandetti case. He had vowed to remember to get his money upfront; that's what retainers were for, right? So the appointment was made, but the new client never showed. When he tried calling, the number turned out to be a pay phone in a public library. Who knew they still had pay phones?

Farman stood on the dark, rickety landing, pondering the demise of payphones and the unreliability of clients while locking the door and deadbolt with his key. He turned to descend the steep, worn wooden stairs down to the alley. Had he turned the other way, he would have faced his killer. Instead, he felt a hard push against his back. As he sprawled downward headfirst, he opened his mouth to scream, but never got it out. It's hard to scream when your neck snaps.

Sam was in Amy's office when the text message came in the next afternoon, right on schedule. It gave the wire instructions and nothing else. Amy did a quick search on her computer.

"As I thought. He's doing this the simplest way possible. He knows you can't bring in law enforcement without implicating yourself, so he's using a major U.S. bank. He's not trying to hide anything."

The name of the account in the wire instructions was Byetower Company. "Can you find out who owns the account?" Sam said. "I mean, considering that Baxter's supposedly dead?"

"Obviously he's pulling your chain. I'll get my researcher to see what we can find out about Byetower."

"You think I should text him back and tell him I won't do it?"

"I don't see what that does for you. If you mean to ignore him, then ignore him."

Another text arrived.

```
You have 5 minutes.
```

Five minutes passed. Ten. Fifteen. Then another message arrived.

```
BIG MISTAKE.
```

Chapter 39

The next afternoon, Rosa answered the knock on Big Vic's front door. The very handsome delivery man with unnaturally blue eyes asked politely if Lisa Gold was home. He needed her to sign for the package.

He'd called her office the day before, posing as a writer who was researching a book on the new generation of Napa vintners. He'd asked the woman who answered the phone if he could set up an interview with Mrs. Gold for the next day. He was told she was not going to be at the winery for at least a few days, but she would be sure Mrs. Gold got his message.

When told she was not currently in residence, which he already knew—he didn't want to kill her, just scare the crap out of her—he smiled warmly and said that he supposed Rosa could sign for it.

Rosa signed where he showed her on his clipboard. As she placed the package on the table in the foyer, it occurred to her that, for some time, she'd signed on electronic devices for deliveries, not on a sheet of paper. But the thought quickly faded.

As they approached the couple's car, Wayne shook hands with the retired dentist from Topeka. He then graciously opened the passenger side door for the man's wife, herself a retired librarian.

After tasting wine and schmoozing with Wayne about how their first trip to California was going, the couple had signed up for the wine club and then asked if they could see how wine was made. They'd just completed what Wayne called his fifty cent tour of Duncan Gold's wine making facility.

The man, a Viet Nam veteran, saluted Wayne before getting in on the driver's side. Wayne returned the acknowledgement.

As he watched them drive off, he noticed a white van pull up and park across the parking lot near Big Vic, with a sign on the side that read, "Local Express." *Another local delivery service,* he thought. *Now there's a growth business.*

Wayne shaded his eyes and watched as the delivery man carried a package to the front door. He watched as the man returned to his van after Rosa took the package. Something about that guy looked familiar, but he couldn't quite put his finger on what it was.

There was no one working at Duncan Gold Vineyards at 2:00 a.m. when the incendiary device went off. It exploded, spewing white-hot phosphorous in all directions. As the old wooden floor and lath walls ignited, the antique wooden table was quickly consumed.

Big Vic had a lot of very old, very dry lumber. She had no sprinkler system, and the fire spread voraciously. Smoke alarms went off in a complaining chorus, but no one heard. The fire detection system did signal the security company, which passed the alert to the local fire department, but by the time they arrived, there was nothing to do but protect the other structures and let the old Victorian burn. When the proud old lady was critically weakened by the inferno, she collapsed with a roar that echoed across the valley like thunder.

The text arrived at 4:00 a.m. This one was sent to both Sam and Lisa.

VERY BIG MISTAKE.

Chapter 40

Our convoy of identical black Escalades motored up I-680 from Silicon Valley to Napa Valley. Lisa and I were in the back seat of the middle car. Kyle Rizzo was driving, and Amy Wu was seated next to him. Each of the other two cars contained two dangerous looking bodyguards.

Lisa had gotten the call about the fire at about 6:00 a.m. That was when she noticed the text message that had come in overnight. She woke me up, and I had never heard such steely resolve in her voice.

I'd left a message for Nora that I wouldn't be in the office and should be called only in the direst emergency. She would work out clearing my calendar.

The atmosphere in our car was funereal. We'd developed our game plan and set the wheels in motion before we'd headed north. Now there was really nothing to say.

Before Amy had arrived that morning, Lisa told me we needed to talk. When she says that, it means I need to listen.

"You need to let me handle this," she said.

"Okay..."

"The thing is, you're great about letting me do my own thing. My event planning business, running the winery, you never meddle. Even when I have tough stuff to handle. You're not a sexist man who needs to take care of the little woman."

"That's just how we are," I said. "We give each other advice, but we don't interfere." I wondered where this was going.

"Except..." she said.

Uh oh. Best to just listen.

"When there's real danger, you jump in and take charge."

I started to protest, but she held up her hand to shut me up.

"I get that you think faster about these things than I do," she said. "You have more experience dealing with legal issues, threats, and all sorts of bad stuff. But when you were lying in that hospital bed, and I had no idea if you'd survive or be disabled or what, I realized something."

I gave Lisa a questioning look.

"I've really always counted on you to protect me from the real bad stuff. To be decisive. But what would happen if you couldn't? What if I had to protect you?"

"You'd need your tiger," I said.

"My tiger needs practice," Lisa said. "And this is as good a time as any to start."

I nodded.

"That doesn't mean we aren't in it together, or that I don't need your help. But I need to be in charge."

I got it. I said so.

Duncan Gold Vineyards was again closed to the public. A sheriff's deputy stopped us at the gate, then waved us through.

Sheriff Jeff Ryder greeted us as we pulled to a stop into the parking lot. "I'm so sorry," he said to Lisa. "They're saying it was arson. But you were lucky. No one was around when it happened; no one was hurt. And there was no wind, so the fire didn't spread."

I heard Mary's voice in my head: *Lucky would be if the device didn't go off...*

But the scene was surreal. Big Vic was a pile of charred rubble surrounded by a fence of sad yellow crime scene tape. But all around, the vineyards and other winery buildings looked almost pristine, as if the fire hadn't happened. There were no other buildings close to Big Vic. That had been intentional, to keep the residence away from the winery activity.

There was still one firetruck and several firefighters standing around, but it was just for show. I'd envisioned smoking wreckage and hotspots bursting into flame, but the fire appeared completely out. Big Vic was dead, a huge mound of charred rubble.

Rosa came running to Lisa and threw her arms around her. "I'm so sorry," she sobbed. "Manuel and I heard a roar, saw the flames. But we could do nothing." Rosa and her husband, Manuel—our all-around winery handyman— lived in a bungalow on the far side of the vineyard.

Lisa comforted Rosa, then huddled with Jeff and the fire marshal. I wandered over to Little Vic, where staff were being interviewed. The old guy who worked part-time in the tasting room approached me. He had a worried look on his face.

"Can I talk to you a minute, Mr. Gold?"

"Sure." I couldn't remember his name. "What is it?"

"Let's walk."

We strolled out into the parking lot. When we were out of earshot of others, he stopped and turned to face me.

"I need to talk to Lisa," he said without preamble. He looked towards the remains of Big Vic. "I know who did it."

Of course, we already knew who did it. And we were going to tell the authorities. We were just waiting for Annie Oakley to arrive. She was in court all day. So Lisa's mission was to stall the fire marshal and sheriff until the evening.

He told me the story of his involvement with Baxter. "Then Baxter dropped me like a hot potato. But I kept coming around. Pretty soon, your wife gave me a job here, which I love. Everyone's so nice to me and I feel useful. Anyway, now this. I can't keep quiet about it, come what may."

"But how do you know Baxter set the fire?"

"I saw him deliver the package yesterday. I mean, I couldn't see his face across the parking lot, but he had the same build, and Baxter's got this hitch in his walk. The delivery guy walked the same way. It was him."

I told him to stroll over to our car and wait there for me. Then I pried Lisa away from the clearly frustrated fire marshal and sheriff—they clearly did not appreciate Lisa stonewalling them. As we walked to the SUV, she told me the old guy's name was Wayne.

Amy and Wayne got into the back seat. I took the passenger seat up front and motioned Amy to the driver's seat. I asked her to turn on the engine, crank up the air conditioning, and close the windows.

I asked Wayne to retell his story. He had difficulty making eye contact with Lisa. When he was done, she reached over and patted his arm.

"It's okay, Wayne. You meant no harm. You were just looking for an adventure."

"But what should I do now?"

"I can't tell you that," Lisa said. "But if I were you, I'd tell the cops what I saw yesterday, just not what I thought it meant. I'd leave any speculation about Baxter out of it. I wouldn't even mention Baxter."

"But..."

"If I were you, I'd leave it to us to figure out what to do with what you've told us about Baxter and you. And I'd assume we'd leave your name out of it."

Wayne nodded thoughtfully. "Then I guess I'll just mosey over and take my turn being interviewed."

Lisa got out of the car and told Jeff and the fire marshal that we were going to get a condo at the Silverado Resort. She'd let them know what our room number was and reiterated that we'd all meet there that evening when Annie arrived.

Chapter 41

Before we headed to Napa Valley that morning, Lisa, Amy and I had met with Sam at his house.

As we drove to Sam's, I called Nick. The plan was Lisa's, but she felt it would be best if I were to ask Nick to play his part. It was barely 7:00 a.m., but Nick was an early riser, so he was clear-headed when I told him what I hoped he'd be willing to do.

"I can do that," he said. "Your wish is my command." He never asked why.

The meeting with Sam was all business. After the events of last night, he knew the game was up.

Lisa had her game face on. No more the sweet, caring woman, she unemotionally but firmly gave him two choices. He could either go along with her plan, or she would be visiting the FBI today with the whole story. Sam chose door A.

Lisa then listed the conditions for her plan. Her manner made it clear there was no room for negotiation. Sam squirmed, but, in the end, he agreed to her terms.

By the time the big powwow started at our condo at the Silverado, Lisa's plan was already in motion.

During our room-service lunch at the condo, she'd had an inspiration about Wayne, and had called him and asked him to drop over. When he arrived and she told him her idea, he was as excited as a little boy with a new bike.

"You know," he said, "Sam was always so darn nice to me. I'm in."

Yes, the wheels were turning.

At Annie's suggestion, Sheriff Jeff Ryder and the fire marshal were joined by a deputy district attorney. Annie figured they might find some legal advice helpful during our discussion.

Annie laid out the ground rules. We would be as forthcoming as possible. She would interrupt only if she thought we were wandering into self-incrimination territory, though she doubted that would happen. She would also stop the proceedings if, as she put it, the conversation started going in the wrong direction.

Since they had no idea what might be coming, our three guests had no choice but to agree.

Lisa took the lead. She laid out everything we knew about Adrian Hightower, Alvin Baxter and the stolen 10 million dollars. At Sam's request, she did not mention Durant. One of Lisa's conditions that morning had been that Sam explain the holes in the story he'd told us. When he'd confessed about Durant's involvement, he plugged them. He had also explained that Durant knew nothing about the stolen money or Baxter. And he had been persuasive that Durant had the resources to hunt him down and kill him anywhere, no matter how well he hid.

Lisa then told them how Adrian Hightower had become Sam Jones, and how the Brandetti shooting had brought Baxter out of the woodwork. Then Amy laid out the threats and demands that had led to last night's fire. We did not mention that we had seen Sam that morning.

Sheriff Ryder and the fire marshal were very quiet during this presentation. This was all clearly out of their realm of experience. The deputy D.A. periodically shook her head in amazement.

Then Annie chimed in. "My investigator and my clients had no reason at first to believe Mr. Jones. Until last night, they thought this might all be some sort of prank or tall tale. But to be on the safe side, Lisa did increase her personal security."

"Nicely played, counsellor," said the deputy D.A., nodding her admiration of the spin.

Amy then handed Jeff a copy of Baxter's file, which now included her investigator's report on the Byetower Company and its bank account. "We believe that Baxter was the one who delivered that package yesterday."

Jeff reached into his attaché case and pulled out a sheet of paper. "This is the sketch our sketch artist made with Rosa today. It doesn't look anything like the photo you have here."

"That's Baxter's driver's license photo," Amy said. "I think that when he staged his death and changed his identity, he got some plastic surgery."

"What about the cell phone he's been texting you with?"

"It's a burner phone, purchased with cash from the Walmart on Lincoln Avenue in Napa," Amy said. "We haven't been able to track it. He probably only turns it on when he sends a text, then occasionally to check for messages. The number's in the file."

The discussion went on for another hour. The lawyers had a few minor lawyerly tiffs, but they were quickly resolved. Wayne's name was never mentioned. Finally, the fire marshal excused himself. "Sheriff, please go catch my arsonist," he said. The others decided it was time to pack it in as well.

Chapter 42

After the sobering session with Lisa, Mike and Amy the morning after the fire, Sam began getting his affairs in order for his vanishing act.

It was mostly computer work. He moved some money around, paid some bills, and did the other sorts of things you might do if you were going on vacation and expected to be off the grid for a while.

Since he was going to soon have a fatal accident, he turned off the triggers that would release the damaging information about General Durant's role in impeding and then containing the Abu Ghraib investigation if he died an unnatural death. It would do him no good to ruin Durant now, and he feared Durant's potential ability to hunt him down and retaliate. It was best that he kept the threat of exposing Durant available to him in case he needed it in his next incarnation.

As he was tidying up loose ends, he came across a Skype phone number he'd stopped using a few months earlier. It was paid for annually and was still active. He'd simple not thought to cancel it. The phone number was the direct line he'd used at Norcal Cash Services. The voicemail was full.

As he listened, he heard the voice that had tormented him in the SUV in the woods just a few nights before.

Over the last two weeks, Julio Trevino had left ever more agitated messages. Trevino had bought Norcal from Sam earlier in the year. His increasingly strident complaint was that, try though he might, he could not even come close to wringing out the amount of profit Sam had made.

Sam remembered explicitly telling Trevino not to count on reproducing the kind of results Norcal's financial reports showed. Of course, he couldn't exactly tell him why, that he had been laundering cash through the business. Trevino had ignored his warning. He'd been dazzled by Norcal's numbers.

"I overpaid you for Norcal," Trevino fairly shouted in one voicemail. "I am making a small profit, but I cannot service the debt."

Norcal had been sold with seller financing. Sam held the note. And he completely understood Trevino's problem.

Sam decided to bail the guy out. The funny thing, he thought, was that part of the reason he wanted to make amends to Trevino—he'd realized back then why Trevino had been willing to overpay for the business and really hadn't tried very hard to dissuade him—was because of how he'd double-crossed Baxter years before.

Adrian Hightower had no idea how to manage money. Born with the proverbial silver spoon in his mouth, money had always been something he spent. He'd never given much thought to where it came from; it was there when he needed it. In the Army, he hadn't needed much money either. So when he became Sam Jones, he'd had a rude awakening.

Oh, sure, he knew he'd need money in his new life. It was the opportunity Baxter's theft had presented that had instigated his plan to start over with a new identity. But he had intended to ultimately give Baxter at least some of the 10 million dollars. When he'd arrived in California and confronted reality, his good intentions quickly faded.

Sam was not a big spender. He lived comfortably but not ostentatiously. Still, it soon became clear that the life he wanted to lead would work out just fine with the 10 million dollar stake he'd appropriated from Baxter. As time passed, it became easier and easier to rationalize that he deserved the money as much as Baxter. There was truly no honor among thieves.

Sam also was able to rationalize his theft by telling himself he was carrying on in the Hightower family tradition. He knew the Hightower fortune had been built on the illegal rum and slave trade that flourished in Newport some 200 years ago. He had heard the elder men telling tales of his ancestors' exploits and laughing about how great fortunes were built on great crimes. Ironically, this was the family legacy he, the great male disappointment, continued.

Now Sam was determined to do something to help Trevino, perhaps if only to convince himself that he wasn't really such a bad guy. He thought about forgiving the loan he'd made that Trevino had used for the deal, but realized that would cause Trevino serious tax problems. The amount forgiven would be treated as income and Trevino would owe a boatload of tax.

So the last thing Sam did that day before leaving on his trip was drop a quitclaim in the mail, signing over his house to Trevino. It was worth at least two million dollars. It was a gift, not taxable to Trevino. Sam's estate would owe gift taxes, because Sam was going to die. He was off to have a fatal accident.

As his security detail drove him to the airport, Sam wondered if the gift to Trevino would somehow balance the cosmic scales of justice a bit. After all, he had two killings on his conscience. Not that they bothered him much. His main objection to killing had always been the danger of getting caught. That and the fact that it was so irrevocable had caused Sam to reject the idea of finding Alvin Baxter and eliminating him. Though having now killed twice, if he had it to do over again, he would have gotten rid of Baxter a long time ago.

He thought about what really happened that day in the vineyard.

They were in the conference room with their lawyers. "Oh, what the hell," Brandetti had said, suddenly jaunty. "Let's take a break and then finish this."

The lawyers had pulled out their phones and waved them away. As they left the barn and started along a path between two rows of vines, Sam's cell phone rang. He looked at the caller ID. "I better take this."

Sam stepped away but Brandetti could still hear some of his end of the conversation. He heard Jones say, "No, it's over. It's time to move on."

When the call ended, Brandetti, unashamed of his eavesdropping, said, "Sounded like you were telling some guy you weren't going to back his startup."

"I only wish," Sam said. "I was telling my ex that he and I were really finished."

"Whatever," Brandetti said. He leaned in close to Jones and smirked. "So it's time for us to put this legal hassle behind us. Don't you agree, Adrian Hightower?"

Sam was stunned. "How..."

"I got a buddy in Texas who's real good at online investigation. I had him do you. Even sent him your fingerprints from a glass you used one time. He taps into all sorts of databases, even military records. And there you were. Adrian Hightower, a guy who vanished ten years ago and reappeared as Sam Jones. I wonder why?"

Sam had never before reacted so quickly. He turned on his heel, sprinted into the barn, and got the gun from the desk drawer where Brandetti kept it. The blowhard had shown it to him once when he was bragging about how he was ready to protect their investment with, in his words, whatever it took.

He ran back outside and confronted Brandetti with the gun, intending to kill him. But Sam was no streetfighter. Instead of shooting right away, he hesitated and got too close. Brandetti grabbed the gun barrel with both hands and wrenched the gun up and out of his hand.

"I've had enough, you queer motherfucker!" he roared, and the chase was on.

In the parking lot moments later, Lisa Gold jumped on Brandetti's back and they fell in a heap on top of Sam, who was badly wounded. Sam grabbed Brandetti's gun hand in both of his hands and managed to twist the weapon so it was pointing towards Brandetti. Still holding Brandetti's hand, he squeezed as hard as he could until the gun went off, killing Brandetti and wounding Lisa.

It was his first kill, Sam thought, but it was self-defense, not murder. Ralph Farman was another story entirely.

When the threats from Baxter began just days ago, it got Sam to thinking that Baxter might have had something to do with the Brandet lawsuit. If so, Baxter might have told Farman about Sam's real identity. Then came the abduction by Trevino, but Sam thought at the time it was Baxter. The physical menace aroused a level of terror that Sam had never before experienced and galvanized him into action. No more Mr. Nice Guy. He vowed from then on that he would permanently and promptly eliminate threats to his well-being.

So he called the lawyer and wheedled out of him that he knew Alvin Baxter. That's all he needed to hear. He made an appointment with the shyster, ditched his security for a few hours, and drove up to Napa. He waited in the dark on the dingy landing for Farman. Then all it took was one good shove, and that risk had been eliminated. Reported as an unfortunate accident, Farman's death merited just three sentences in the "roundup" section of the local Napa newspaper.

With two kills under his belt, Sam found he liked the finality they brought to problems. So he decided to hunt Baxter down and end that problem once and for all. But events had rapidly taken over, and Lisa Gold—unaware of Sam's killings—had come up with an even better plan.

When they arrived at San Jose International, Sam dismissed his security detail, thanked them, and told them he wouldn't need them again until he returned from vacation.

Before he boarded his flight, Sam called his doctor's office. He told the receptionist that he was experiencing a little dizziness, maybe even some vertigo. It was probably, he said, something to do with the shooting incident. No, he didn't think it was an emergency. He scheduled an appointment in 10 days' time.

He caught a Southwest flight from San Jose to San Diego, where he was met at the airport by Emilio Fuentes. Fuentes was a Mexican freelance private investigator who did work from time to time for Kowalski-Wu Investigations.

During the two hour drive to Ensenada, Fuentes briefed Sam on the details of the Mexican portion of Lisa's plan. Sam listened attentively. If you wanted to survive a fatal accident, you had to pay careful attention to details.

When they arrived in Ensenada, Fuentes dropped Sam at a mid-priced motel near the fishing docks. As he checked in for a week's stay, Sam mentioned to the young woman at reception that he was planning to get some alone time and do some fishing. Her English was good, but she thought "alone time" was a funny phrase.

Fuentes picked Sam up at 6:00 a.m. Fuentes was dressed in his local fishing guide outfit: worn hoodie, jeans and sneakers. Sam wore his American tourist outfit: San Francisco Giants baseball cap, sweatshirt and windbreaker, along with jeans and sneakers.

Minutes later, they arrived at the sport fishing docks. Using Sam's credit card, Fuentes rented a small outboard boat for his customer. When they got to the boat, they had a loud, heated argument, during which Fuentes waved his hands vigorously. Though the dock was not crowded, several local fisherman heard Fuentes shout something about safety and the danger of fishing on the ocean alone.

As Sam unhitched the lines and eased the boat away from the dock, an obviously exasperated Fuentes stormed off, muttering to himself in disgust. As he passed the boat rental kiosk on the way to his car, he told the rental agent that he was washing his hands of the crazy gringo. "The lunatic wants to go out by himself," he said in his native Spanish. "Says he needs alone time, whatever the hell that is."

His role played to perfection, Fuentes drove off.

The capsized boat was found at about 9:00 a.m., when it was noticed by the captain of a fishing charter heading out for a day of deep-sea fishing with a group of tourists. It was several miles out in the Pacific Ocean, in an area known for unpredictable currents and waves.

Fishing gear and a San Francisco Giants baseball cap were found floating nearby. The body of the tourist who rented the boat and wanted alone time was never found.

When he was Adrian Hightower, Sam Jones had spent a good deal of time boating. It was what those in his social class did. But he'd never gone fishing, and his record remained intact.

Chapter 43

While Sam Jones was boating to his demise, Sheriff Ryder was assigning Detective Susan Escobar to the arson case. He gave her Amy's file on Baxter, Rosa's sketch and Wayne's description of the van.

"I've started a case with less," she said. "Maybe forensics will get lucky with the device."

Forensics had no such luck. The device was at the center of a very hot fire. They could dope out what kind of a device it was, but there was nothing to identify where any of its easily available components came from. Plus there were instructions on how to build it all over the internet, even step-by-step videos.

The description the witness Wayne provided of the van turned out to be crucial. Because the van had to turn around to leave the parking lot, he had seen Local Express signs on both sides. The one on the passenger side was a little crooked. Wayne had suggested it was probably a magnetic sign.

So Detective Escobar started checking rental agencies. The two ladies who worked the counter at the local Enterprise Rent-A-Car recognized the sketch as that of the very handsome man with unnaturally blue eyes who had rented a white van the day before the fire. The younger one remembered him because he looked so dreamy. The older one remembered him because of his weird name.

"Dirk Clark, for god's sake. What the hell kind of goofy name is that?"

She quickly retrieved his rental agreement, complete with credit card and driver's license information; you could not rent a vehicle without providing both.

The magnetic sign helped nail the lead down. Sure, you could order one online, and there were dozens of places within an easy drive where you could get one made, but Escobar assumed Clark had been in a hurry. So she started by checking the sign shops closest to the rental office. On her third try, the sales clerk vividly remembered the very handsome man with unnaturally blue eyes. Paid cash, paid extra for same-day service.

Escobar congratulated herself on her day's work. With the van and the sign, she knew she had her arsonist. She had his name, picture, credit card, driver's license number and bank account. It wouldn't be long before she'd nail this guy.

Now all she had to do is find him. She had no idea that she'd soon be getting help from a usually unhelpful source.

Chapter 44

Shortly after he'd given the case to Detective Escobar, Jeff Ryder took a phone call from FBI Special Agent in Charge Alex Greene.

"I just got off a weird phone call from Mike Gold. It was very cryptic. He said you might have some information for me about the theft of some of Saddam Hussein's money during the Iraq war."

The last time Ryder had worked with Greene, they had captured contract killer, serial killer and financial swindler Benjamin Baggs at Duncan Gold Vineyards. Just before he was apprehended, Baggs had been chasing Mike Gold through the winery and shooting at him. As Greene waited for Ryder to reply, he marveled at the similarity of that incident to the recent Lisa Gold shooting.

As if reading Greene's mind, Ryder said, "Those two are quite a pair, aren't they?"

"That they are."

"Well, let me tell you what I got," Ryder said.

After he finished briefing Greene, Ryder said, "My priority is my arson case. We're focusing on Baxter. I doubt we'll get around to Jones for a while."

"Okay," said Greene. "How about we help you look for Baxter. We can amp up the search nationwide. Meanwhile, we'll talk to Jones. He's central to what appears to be our new case."

"At this point," said Ryder, "we'd mainly like to hear Jones's version of what's gone on since the shooting, the stuff that led up to the arson. That's *our* case. And I'm sure Indiana would like to talk to him about that safe robbery. As for Baxter, he's probably nearby. He doesn't even know we're looking at him for the arson. Let's not spook him."

"We really need Baxter for our case," said Greene. "But we can probably wait a few days before we go nationwide. We'll focus on Jones first. I'll be sure we get what you need when we interview him about the Iraqi loot, and we'll share it with you."

"The FBI sharing? Be still my heart!" said Ryder.

"Whatever," said Greene.

Ryder chuckled. "There is one thing that would really help us. Baxter's been using a burner phone to send text messages. We can't track it; he doesn't keep it on long enough. But I bet you guys have the ability to keep pinging it to locate it when it does come on."

"I bet we do, too. Will the number be in the file you send us?"

"Sure. We hick town sheriffs share too."

But Sam Jones was nowhere to be found. By noon, the FBI had tracked his movements to Ensenada—he'd left more breadcrumbs to follow than Hansel and Gretel—where the local authorities had already chalked up his death to the carelessness of yet another foolhardy, arrogant gringo tourist.

As Greene listened to his agent's report about Jones, he thought about how the Pacific Ocean had been an even better place for Jones's body to disappear than the Mississippi River had been for Baxter's.

Chapter 45

The day after the fire, Dirk Clark was agitated.

Building the device had been easy. He'd gotten the first month's rent on the mini-storage unit for a dollar! He bought all the materials at Home Depot and an agriculture supply store and just followed the instructions in the YouTube video.

The fire had gone as planned. He'd once seen a show on TV where the arsonist had insisted that someone sign for the package, to be sure it would get inside where it could do the most damage, and not just sit on the porch. He'd overlooked the fact that the housekeeper would get a very good look at his face. It had occurred to him that she might get caught in the fire, but then he put that out of his mind. He didn't know that she and her husband lived on the Duncan Gold property; when he'd been casing out the place, she'd been staying in Big Vic in order to help the recuperating Sam Jones.

But now he could not understand why Jones hadn't wired the money. Why hadn't he or Lisa Gold at least responded to his text? What did he have to do to get these people's attention?

All morning, he'd been anxiously checking for messages, then popping the battery out of his phone so it couldn't be tracked. It was a pain in the ass, waiting for the phone to boot up each time. And with Jones's stonewalling, he was distressed about his remaining options.

He looked over his list for the umpteenth time that morning. Each remaining option involved physical violence and significant risk. He believed he had the stomach for the violence, it was the risk that troubled him. Still, it was *his* 10 million bucks.

The burger and fries he'd had for lunch were jumping around in his gut. He needed a distraction to settle his nerves. So he decided to watch *Butch Cassidy and the Sundance Kid;* doing that always made him feel good. And now he thought he looked a bit like a cross between Newman and Redford.

While he watched, he thought about the way Butch and Sundance helped each other and had so much fun together. He wondered if he would be better off with a partner. It wasn't too late to do that, and he could sure use another pair of hands, and, for that matter, another head.

Nah, I'm a loner. Always have been. That's why he was able to steal the money in the first place. It was why he was able to keep it hidden for so long. He didn't have to worry about a partner cheating him or getting cold feet or letting something slip out when he was drunk.

Hightower ripping him off proved it was better to go it alone. Plus he had never been good at sharing, and, except when he was hustling a chick to get laid, other people mainly annoyed him.

He felt himself getting riled up again. He grabbed a beer out of the cooler, opened a bag of Doritos, and let himself get lost in the adventures of Butch and Sundance.

When the movie was over, Dirk popped open his fourth beer of the day. He was feeling a lot better. He figured time was on his side, so he wouldn't panic and do something rash.

He left the TV on with the volume muted and popped the battery back in his phone. As it was booting up, he saw BREAKING NEWS flash across the bottom of the screen. A pretty reporter with a serious expression stood in front of a mound of charred rubble with a vineyard in the background. Dirk turned up the volume.

"Last night, fire destroyed the home of Lisa and Mike Gold at their Napa Valley winery, Duncan Gold Vineyards. Authorities tell us they are conducting an arson investigation. Fortunately, no one was in the stately Victorian mansion as it was consumed in the inferno."

A distance shot of an open boat on some body of water came on the screen. "And this just in. Police in Ensenada, Mexico have confirmed that Sam Jones is assumed dead in a boating accident this morning. It appears that Jones was fishing alone in treacherous Pacific waters when his rented boat capsized. His body was not recovered."

Side-by-side head shots of Lisa and Sam replaced the stock boat shot. "You may recall that, earlier this year, Lisa Gold saved Sam Jones's life when she stopped Giuseppe Brandetti from killing him. During that altercation at Brandetti's Napa Valley winery, Jones was shot three times and Brandetti shot himself and died. Lisa Gold was wounded by the same bullet that killed Brandetti."

A close up shot of the pretty reporter with the serious expression filled the screen. "We have no reason at this time to believe that last night's fire and Jones's fatal accident are connected. For now, this appears to be just a bizarre coincidence."

Dirk turned off the TV. It had never occurred to him that Sam Jones would die. *What now?*

Two more beers later, Dirk had still not figured out what to do next. Was he really out of options to get his 10 million dollars back? Then an idea burst through his beery fog. What if Jones had done a disappearing act, like he had? A loud knock on his motel room door interrupted this inspiration.

"Open up. This is the police. We have the building surrounded."

As she took Alvin Baxter, alias Dirk Clark, into custody, Detective Susan Escobar had a big grin on her face. The doofus had turned his phone on over a half-hour ago and left it on. An FBI tech—she had no idea where he was located—called her on her cell phone and led her and two black-and-whites right to Baxter's door. It turned out that sometimes the FBI did share.

Chapter 46

When General Mackenzie Durant heard about Sam Jones's death, it took him a good half hour and three stiff bourbons to calm himself enough to think clearly. Or as clearly as you could after three stiff bourbons in a half hour.

His concern was that the damning documentation of his role in the Abu Ghraib investigation, that Adrian Hightower had shown him on that flash drive all those years ago, would now be released. Hightower had been unambiguous. If he died of anything but a natural cause— an illness or old age—copies of that damn drive would be sent to several news outlets. Death by drowning was hardly a natural cause.

That threat had hung over his head for 10 years. All Jones asked was that Durant keep his identity change a secret. He had asked for nothing else until the Brandetti shooting. Then he had asked for some protection, but only for a little while.

Over the years, Durant had gotten used to the dormant threat. He couldn't have Sam Jones guarded 24/7, and there was no reasonable way to protect him from the danger of an unnatural death.

Threatening Jones wouldn't work. All Jones would have to do is say, "Screw you, you threaten me or hurt me in any way and I'll release the flash drives. What's on them doesn't do me any damage."

After he had ascended to the number two position in Army Intelligence, he had considered using all his resources to find out where Jones had hidden the copies of that flash drive and how he had set up the trigger mechanism to release them if he died an unnatural death. But he couldn't be sure his efforts would turn up all of the copies and all of the triggers.

So Durant had pretty much forgotten about the whole thing. Secrets were his business—finding them, keeping them, using them—his closet was full of secrets, many of which could threaten his own wellbeing. This was just another one. That is, until the Brandetti shooting. That was a reality shock treatment. Since then, he had been thinking more and more about helping Sam Jones die a natural death, or what would appear to be one. He was getting ready to put that in motion when the queer little bastard went off and drowned.

Durant had assigned an agent to check on the incident. Jones had done what any normal person would do to prepare for a vacation. He'd flown commercial and booked a room under his own name. He'd told the clerk at motel reception he wanted some time to himself. They couldn't locate the guide he had hired, but it looked like once he had made the arrangements for the boat, Sam had dismissed him and gone fishing by himself. Not a smart move in the tricky Pacific waters off Ensenada.

The lack of a body was a loose end, but, according to his field agent, not a surprise in those waters.

So now I just wait for the other shoe to drop, he thought. Better have another bourbon.

Chapter 47

The phone call to Tulula was brief but friendly. When he told Manville's secretary that Vic King was calling, Nick Marchetti was put through to Rick Manville right away.

"Mr. King," Manville said, "it's been a while. You left us rather suddenly."

Vic King reminded Manville about the two rather persuasive men who had visited shortly after he'd last left Tulula, the men who had explained to Manville about the Amanda Miller problem. "Let's just say that they are associates of mine," he said.

That surprised Manville, but also explained a few things. It certainly got his undivided attention. "What can I do for you, Mr. King?"

He explained. Manville was quite agreeable.

The Gulfstream rolled to a stop at Faleolo International Airport in Samoa. As the stairs came down, a white S-Class Mercedes rolled up, the driver got out and opened the rear passenger-side door, and Rick Manville stepped out. The door to the aircraft opened, and Vic King descended to the tarmac.

The two men shook hands like long lost friends. Then Manville climbed the stairs, followed by King.

As he entered the sumptuous cabin, Manville took in the two men who rose from their plush leather seats. One was tall, thin and elderly, though he had a full head of gray hair and a twinkle in his blue eyes. The other was on the short side, with just a stubble of hair on his head, warm brown eyes, and a pale face. Manville did not know that the shorter man had just recently stopped shaving his head and started shaving his face.

"So, Mr. King, these are my new friends," Manville said.

"Name's Wayne," said the old man, offering his hand. His grip was surprisingly firm.

The other man extended his hand. "I'm what you might call between names," he said. "But as soon as I have a new one and open a bank account, Vic here will be sending me a substantial sum of money. It's my own money that he's sort of taking care of for a while."

Manville nodded. "And then you'll be buying one of my villas?"

"I will. And Wayne and I were thinking of opening a wine bar together."

"Come, my friends, let me take you to my lovely village of Tulula." Looking at Sam, Manville said, "Then we can get you *your* new alias."

Epilogue

"Thank you all so much for coming. Today we are breaking ground for the Sam Jones Physical Therapy Center."

Lisa looked up at the cloudless sky as she continued. "We are all hoping that there are many construction delays due to rain this winter." This brought the expected laughter, but it was tinged with the anxiety we were all feeling as the severe drought entered its fifth year.

"The entire cost of this facility and property was donated by Sam Jones just before he died in that terrible accident." Pointing to Janelle in the front row, she said, "He told me we have you, Janelle, to thank for his interest in physical therapy. Though he did refer to you as his torturer." This time, the laughter was more wholehearted.

"Sam loved the Napa Valley and the people he encountered in our wine industry." When she'd read her speech to Mike, he'd suggested that Sam had perhaps not loved Giuseppe Brandetti; Lisa said Brandetti didn't count as part of the Napa wine industry. "He wanted a place where all of those who worked in the vineyards or making wine could receive the best possible physical therapy when they needed it, regardless of their ability to pay."

Lisa turned and pointed to the large artist's rendition of what the building would look like. "This is Sam's legacy."

While Washington D.C. lay covered in white by a mid-January snowstorm, the head of U.S. Army Intelligence formally announced her expected retirement.

Before a successor could be nominated, California Senator Sonya Rivera let the president's chief-of-staff know that she would oppose the elevation of General Mackenzie Durant to that position. No reason was given.

General Durant, who had been quietly celebrating his apparent reprieve from the Sam Jones threat—the other shoe had never dropped—and his imminent ascension to the pinnacle of U.S. Army Intelligence, was shocked when he was informed he would be passed over for the promotion.

Lisa and I were in Bend, Oregon, for one of our quick weekend getaways. We were sitting on the front porch of the cabin we'd rented when Lisa noticed a small item in the newspaper about the retirements of the head of U.S. Army Intelligence and her deputy, unusual in that both occurred in the same week.

"You know anything about this?" she said, showing me the article.

"I might have mentioned something to the Senator," I said. *Mr. Innocent.*

"That wasn't part of the plan," Lisa said, raising her right eyebrow in challenge.

"Well, I just..."

Alias

"You just can't help yourself, can you?" she said with a sigh.

Author's Note

This novel uses historical events from the Iraq war to create a fictional story. All its characters are completely fictional. In particular, the following characters in this book related to events in Iraq are specifically and exclusively the products of my imagination: the unnamed Whistleblower of Abu Ghraib, Mackenzie Durant, Adrian Hightower/Sam Jones, and Alvin Baxter.

In March 2003, the United States and its coalition partners invaded Iraq. Later that year, Amnesty International and the Associated Press reported that U.S. Army soldiers and CIA agents had been committing human rights violations against prisoners in the Abu Ghraib prison. These allegations ultimately led to investigations that revealed acts of torture, rape, sodomy and murder. However, the initial reports received little attention.

On January 16, 2004, the U.S. Command in Baghdad issued a one-paragraph press release: "An investigation has been initiated into reported incidents of detainee abuse at a Coalition Forces detention facility. The release of specific information concerning the incidents could hinder the investigation, which is in its early stages. The investigation will be conducted in a thorough and professional manner."

In this novel, I have taken the artistic liberty of attributing this press release to my fictional character Colonel Durant.

The press release received little notice. Then on April 28, 2004, *60 Minutes II* aired a segment showing photos of U.S. Army guards posing with big grins next to hooded, naked Iraqi prisoners. The graphic images caused the floodgates of reporting to open worldwide. In this novel, I attributed the TV show to *60 Minutes* instead of *60 Minutes II* to make the narrative simpler.

Between May 2004 and March 2006, eleven soldiers were court martialed for dereliction of duty and other charges related to prisoner abuse at Abu Ghraib. They were convicted, imprisoned, and ultimately dishonorably discharged. Prison terms ranged from several months to 10 years. Other military personnel were reprimanded and some were reduced in rank. No one was charged with the murders that were uncovered.

The most senior U.S. Army officer punished was Brigadier General Janis Karpinski, who had been commanding officer at Abu Ghraib. She was demoted to the rank of colonel. More senior U.S. Army officers in the chain of command were not disciplined.

In its final report, the Independent Panel to Review Department of Defense Detention Operations said: "The Panel finds no evidence that organizations above the 800th MP brigade or the 205th MI Brigade-level were directly involved in the incidents at Abu Ghraib." Thus the buck stopped well down the chain of command, and Justice Department, CIA and DOD leadership were completely off the hook.

Sergeant Joseph Darby was the real Whistleblower of Abu Ghraib. He was an M.P. who came across damning photos quite by accident when he borrowed a friend's camera. His conscience led him to turn over the photos to a CID investigator. He was promised anonymity, but that evaporated when a New Yorker article revealed his name and Defense Secretary Donald Rumsfeld trumpeted it at a Senate hearing. Darby and his wife felt threatened when they returned to their hometown in Maryland and were relocated to a secret location under military protective custody. Darby later gave a number of press and TV interviews. The unnamed Whistleblower of Abu Ghraib character in this book is loosely based on the events surrounding Mr. Darby, but is a fictional character contrived to help tell the story I made up.

Everything about Durant and Hightower/Jones in this book is fictional. There is no evidence that CID did anything other than a thorough and proper job of investigating the Abu Ghraib scandal. There is no evidence that there was foot-dragging, interference or any attempt to limit the scope of the investigation.

As for Saddam Hussein's cash hoard, on December 3, 2003, *ABC News* reported that over a billion dollars in cash had been removed from the Iraqi Central Bank just hours before the bombing of Baghdad began. A handwritten note was found in the bank's files that the news report translated as follows:

Extremely confidential. In the name of God the most merciful the most compassionate. Mr. Governor of the Iraqi central bank. We are giving, with this written note, permission to Mr. Qusay Saddam Hussein and Mr. Hekmat Mizban Ibrahiem to receive the following amounts of money:

1-Nine hundred and twenty million American dollars.
2-Ninety million Euros.

To protect and save them from American aggression. Take the necessary action.

(signed) Saddam Hussein, President of the Republic

This was the note I quoted in this book.

The *ABC News* report further described the cash as being stored in stainless steel briefcases, one million to two million dollars/euros per case. It states that U.S. forces recovered most of the cash, but 132 million dollars in $100 bills remained missing and were assumed to be in the hands of insurgents.

There is no evidence that any U.S. Army personnel were involved in stealing the missing cash. I invented the character of Alvin Baxter, his theft of the money, and his connection to Abu Ghraib and Hightower/Jones because it made for good fiction.

Acknowledgements

I want to again thank my wonderful editorial staff, Lois Bookman and Judy Reed.

Lois, my wife, suffers through my writing frenzies with equanimity. She is always supportive and enthusiastic about my literary work. More, she is a superb editor, homing in on weak areas of the plot and character development with pinpoint suggestions for improvement. The fit and finish of my novels are largely due to her.

Sister-in-law Judy is my grammarian *par excellence*. She catches what Microsoft Word misses. I appreciate her patience, thoroughness and support.

And to my readers, my thanks. Your feedback is both motivating and valuable. I love hearing what you like and dislike, and your comments inevitably influence my story telling. I especially appreciate those of you who take the time to write reviews on Amazon.

Contact me at philtheauthor@outlook.com

Visit my author page at philbookman.com

Silicon Valley Billionaire Murder!

Opium
Mike Gold Mystery Book 1
by Phil Bookman

O-P-M: Other People's Money
It's the food that nourishes tech startups. O-P-M. Other People's Money. To many entrepreneurs in Silicon Valley, it's known irreverently as opium, because once you get on it, it's hard to kick the habit. Silicon Valley software entrepreneur Mike Gold is an expert at using this opium to fund his startups.

Mike is between ventures and getting antsy when he's offered an intriguing proposition: start up a new company funded by billionaire tech icon Barry Samson. But when Samson is found murdered, and Gold's friends start disappearing, the FBI targets him as a suspect.

To protect his family, his reputation, and his freedom, Mike has to unravel a puzzle involving his best friends, buried events from his childhood, mysterious women, and retired mobsters. And he better move fast, because the FBI is after him and time is running out.

February 2009: First in the Mike Gold Mystery Series
Available at Amazon.com

Biotech Thriller!

Charisma
Mike Gold Mystery Book 2
by Phil Bookman

What is the dark side of charisma?

When Hollywood science celebrity Abe Wiezman invites Silicon Valley software entrepreneur Mike Gold to become CEO of his eight-year-old biotech company, Mike is intrigued. Abe's messianic belief that the company can save the world from pollution and maybe even from global warming is intoxicating.

As he dives into the challenges of learning new technology and taking the company public, Mike discovers some of the downsides of running an organization built around a charismatic personality. But these management problems fade into the background when Abe starts receiving death threats. Then those threats escalate into violence that puts the lives of Abe, Mike and his son in peril. To save them, Mike has to face down his own demons in ways he never imagined. In the process, he discovers the real dark side of charisma.

March 2010: Second in the Mike Gold Mystery Series
Available at Amazon.com

Murder in the Vineyards!

Riding the Tiger
Mike Gold Mystery Book 3
by Phil Bookman

How do you get off the tiger without being eaten?
When Silicon Valley entrepreneur Mike Gold's plans for an IPO falter, his old college buddy Stew King calls out of the blue with a great offer to buy Mike's company. They meet for a quiet weekend at Mike's Napa Valley winery to negotiate the sale. But this is hardly an ordinary business deal. Mike soon discovers that the White House is behind it, the Chinese want to scuttle it, and the ecology of a million square miles of ocean may be at stake.

Then the body of a beautiful, seductive woman is found in the vineyard and Mike is arrested for her murder. With his freedom and maybe his life at risk, Mike uses all his resources to try to discover who framed him and why. When he gets too close to the answer, his beloved Lisa is kidnapped to lure him to a life or death showdown with ruthless killers.

February 2011: Third in the Mike Gold Mystery Series
Available at Amazon.com

Silicon Valley Thriller!

Slice
Mike Gold Mystery Book 4
by Phil Bookman

Pizza, technology, murder and scandal!
Zack Zander, billionaire CEO and founder of MySlice, is on top of the world. Silicon Valley's hottest tech company, MySlice is an ingenious marriage of a pizza chain with social media. But then Zack and three senior executives are savagely murdered onboard his yacht.

Lounging in a villa in Maui, Mike Gold is asked to take over as MySlice CEO. He relishes the challenges of rebuilding the executive team, calming dismayed employees and soothing the financial markets. But the murders don't stop, and as the body count climbs, Mike wonders who he can trust and who is killing MySlice executives.

As he rushes to find the answers in order to stem the tide of negative publicity swirling around his company, Mike uncovers a secret that could destroy MySlice and derail the presidential ambitions of the nation's hottest politician. But his clever plan to deal with this mess literally explodes in his face.

May 2015: Fourth in the Mike Gold Mystery Series
Available at Amazon.com

A lover of mystery novels, Silicon Valley tech veteran Phil Bookman decided the world needed a mystery series featuring a high tech CEO hero. Thus came the Mike Gold Mystery Series. Mike is a great tech CEO, but trouble seems to find him with alarming regularity. Phil's life is not nearly as exciting as Mike's.

Phil grew up in Seaford, New York, where he met and married his high school sweetheart, Lois. He has degrees from Rensselaer Polytechnic Institute, Adelphi University and Santa Clara University. Lois and Phil reside in Los Gatos, California and have lived in Silicon Valley since 1974. Phil had a long career as a software entrepreneur, starting a number of successful software companies.

Contact Phil at philtheauthor@outlook.com

Visit Phil's author page at philbookman.com

All Phil's books are available on Amazon.com